Monica heard a strange buzzing sound…

She focused on the noise, trying to figure out what it was. It kind of sounded like a car engine, but it wasn't coming from the direction of the driveway.

She turned to Kris. By his unmoving stance and the expression of concentration on his face, she knew he heard it, too. "What could that be?"

Kris darted to the wall and hit the switch to kill the kitchen lights, hiding them in darkness. Then he moved toward the kitchen window to move aside the blind and look outside.

Boom!

The sound was both a roar and a hideous crushing noise, combined with an impact that shook the house to its foundation.

Kris launched himself atop Monica, taking them both to the floor as a hot cloud of wood and concrete debris shot through the still-shuddering house…

Jenna Night comes from a family of Southern-born natural storytellers. Her parents were avid readers and the house was always filled with books. No wonder she grew up wanting to tell her own stories. She's lived on both coasts but currently resides in the Inland Northwest, where she's astonished by the occasional glimpse of a moose, a herd of elk or a soaring eagle.

Books by Jenna Night

Love Inspired Suspense

Big Sky First Responders

Deadly Ranch Hideout

Range River Bounty Hunters

Abduction in the Dark
Fugitive Ambush
Mistaken Twin Target
Fugitive in Hiding

Rock Solid Bounty Hunters

Fugitive Chase
Hostage Pursuit
Cold Case Manhunt

Visit the Author Profile page at LoveInspired.com for more titles.

Deadly Ranch Hideout

JENNA NIGHT

LOVE INSPIRED SUSPENSE
INSPIRATIONAL ROMANCE

LOVE INSPIRED® SUSPENSE
INSPIRATIONAL ROMANCE

Recycling programs for this product may not exist in your area.

ISBN-13: 978-1-335-63817-5

Deadly Ranch Hideout

Copyright © 2024 by Virginia Niten

For questions and comments about the quality of this book, please contact us at CustomerService@Harlequin.com.

® is a trademark of Harlequin Enterprises ULC.

Love Inspired
22 Adelaide St. West, 41st Floor
Toronto, Ontario M5H 4E3, Canada
www.LoveInspired.com

Printed in Lithuania

MIX
Paper | Supporting responsible forestry
FSC® C021394

For where your treasure is,
there will your heart be also.
—*Matthew* 6:21

To my mom, Esther.
I look forward to seeing you again.

ONE

Monica Larson stared in horror as the black SUV holding her father burst into flames with a bone-rattling *bang*!

The windows blew out, and chunks of safety glass rained down onto the asphalt of the Reno street like a shower of frosty hail. Car alarms blared in both directions along the road.

She stood on the sidewalk across the street with every muscle in her torso knotted up in terror, while at the same time the bones and joints of her legs seemed to melt and her stance became unsteady.

Following the rush of incoming air from the vehicle's broken windows, the flames *whooshed* and flared outside of the SUV, reaching even farther and higher into the sky.

A chunk of metal slammed to the ground by Monica's feet, sending up a spray of debris and snapping her out of her shocked stupor.

"Dad!"

She pulled herself together and was finally able to move. As she sprinted across the street toward the smoke and heat, her attention remained laser-focused on rescuing her father. *He could still be alive*, she told herself repeatedly, forcing her legs to pump as fast as possible. *There's still a chance.*

Grief and fear squeezed her throat, making it a fight to breathe. She stumbled over her clumsy feet and fell, barely feeling the pain as she scraped a layer of skin from her chin and the palms of her hands. Crumpled on the ground, she heard a second explosion, and looked up in time to see the SUV lift slightly off the ground before it dropped back to the street as another fireball shot from the vehicle and up into the sky.

"No!"

She tried to shove herself back onto her feet, but was derailed by a fit of coughing and gasping as she was nearly overcome by the black, oily smoke roiling toward her.

And then she jerked awake.

After several disoriented seconds ticked by, the impression so strong in her mind that it seemed as if she still smelled the smoke, she began to focus on unfamiliar objects in the darkness of the room where she lay in a sleeping bag atop the lumpy mattress of a bed.

"He's still alive," she whispered to herself, her

chest knotted with grief from what she'd seen happen to her dad in the dream. "It wasn't real."

She focused on her breathing, trying to slow it down while sending up a short, brief prayer and reminding herself that right here, right now, she was okay. It was a well-established routine after she'd gotten so much experience grappling with the sudden wallop of panic that often woke her out of a sound sleep. Turned out that witnessing your accountant father being arrested and finding out that he'd been working for an organized crime group for *years* and later seeing him locked up in prison could do some emotional damage to a mobster bookkeeper's daughter.

And then there was the fallout that came *after* her father's imprisonment.

Maybe it was a good thing she couldn't remember some of the more recent events. She rubbed her fingers along the right side of her head, feeling the ridges hidden by her hair where her stitches would completely dissolve eventually. She tried to think back to that missing gap of time after she'd gone to visit her dad in prison and then woken up in the hospital. A car crash, she'd been told, had caused the cuts and bruises and a state of unconsciousness that had apparently lasted for several hours.

She'd been blessed not to suffer major physical injury or significant brain damage, except for the loss of the memory of that short gap of time between going to visit her dad and waking up in the hospital. That was still gone. She might regain it, she'd been told. Then again, she might not. Right now all she had was the impression that the memory was almost in her grasp, like the feeling she typically had just before she recalled a word or fact that was on the tip of her tongue. Her father had been involved in a physical altercation immediately after her visit, and for that reason she was not allowed to call or visit him for the next month.

What she *did* have was the voice memo she'd left for herself on her phone. She'd discovered it shortly after leaving the hospital, and apparently she'd recorded it during that mystery gap of time. It was the reason she'd left her home in Reno, Nevada, and come up here to Cedar Lodge, Montana, to this unfamiliar and rustic cabin outside of town.

Creak.

The sound came through the open bedroom door from the direction of the kitchen. She'd arrived around midnight after a long and tiresome drive. She'd unrolled her sleeping bag atop the bed, climbed in while still dressed in jeans and a T-shirt, and immediately fallen into a deep sleep until the nightmare had woken her up.

"Probably just a raccoon," she told herself, wanting desperately to believe that.

But pretending something wasn't happening didn't make it go away. She knew that only too well.

And right now, the smarter part of herself, the part determined to survive, had already shot adrenaline through her system and sent her heart racing.

Should she switch on the bedside light? Would that scare away an intruder if there was one or make her an easier target?

Creak.

The sound was definitely coming from the kitchen. Maybe it was a normal noise, like the timber of the old building shifting or the refrigerator cycling on or off. Monica did not want to call the police if she could avoid it. Staying clear of them was included in her plan to keep a low profile while she was here.

She got out of the sleeping bag, dropped her feet to the cold wooden floor and slid them into her shoes.

She was reaching for her phone and key fob when she realized she smelled smoke. *For real.* It wasn't just a lingering impression from her dream.

Her mind raced as she hurried out of the bedroom. She'd been exhausted when she'd arrived after the long drive from Reno. Had she put something on the stove or in the toaster oven and forgotten about it?

Smoke pushed through the gap under the swinging door between the living room and the kitchen. The cabin was old, and Monica could imagine it burning to the ground well before a fire engine could get here.

She grabbed her phone from her pocket, ready to call 9-1-1 if she needed to.

Shoving open the door, she spotted the fire in the dining nook between the refrigerator and the back door. Something was burning beneath the dining table; the table was already engulfed, and flames were crawling up the nearby wall and toward the door.

Pulling the front of her shirt up over her nose to filter some of the smoke, Monica hurried toward the cabinets, hoping to find a pitcher or large bowl that she could fill with water and then douse the flames. Through the fabric she caught a whiff of a familiar yet out-of-place smell.

Gasoline.

Her eyes darted toward the rapidly burning table and what must be gasoline-soaked wood or cloth burning beneath it.

Confirmation that this was not some accidental fire caused by forgetfulness on her part or old faulty wiring. This was intentionally set.

They've found me. The realization chilled her despite the heat.

In the next instant, someone grabbed her from behind and shoved her toward the fire.

They want to kill me and make it look like an accident!

Her father's former criminal bosses must have sent one of their hit men to finish her off as some sort of punishment directed at her dad. Or else the attacker had been hired by Archer Nolan, also employed by the mob, though Monica hadn't been able to prove that fact. Yet. Archer had Monica's mom, Suzanne, convinced that he was a legitimate businessman, and two weeks ago, Suzanne had agreed to marry him in a month. That meant the wedding would happen in two weeks. Monica's mother refused to believe that the man who'd offered her so much comfort after her ex-husband was arrested could also be a criminal when Monica had told her that was the case. Suzanne demanded proof.

Monica was determined to find it. She had to save her mom and protect her family. It was why she'd come to Cedar Lodge.

But right now she was fighting for her life. The heavyset thug who'd grabbed her knocked the phone out of her hand and held her arms pinned to her sides as he continued forcing her toward the flames.

Monica twisted her body as hard as she could, desperate to break free. But it did no good. The masked assailant gripped her tighter, his overwhelming strength enough to propel her forward. She pulled up her feet, hoping the sudden full weight of her body would throw the attacker off balance, but it made no difference.

Lord, help!

The flames were growing, and her face was getting hot.

She fought the thug with every bit of strength she had, but there wasn't much she could do other than twist and stomp her feet back toward him. Unexpectedly, the attacker let go of her arms. But in the next instant he grabbed her neck and began squeezing.

Panic shot through her. She clawed at his hands, but her air supply was already being cut off, and the flaming kitchen began to spin around her. Once she lost consciousness, it would all be over, for good.

Gritting her teeth, she grunted and kicked her heel backward as hard as she could, connecting with his shin. Desperate for a weapon, she dug her hand into her front pocket for the key chain attached to her car fob. It had a couple of metal keys on it, and she slid them between her fingers so they were protruding like a knife point. She clenched to make a fist.

The attacker was so close behind her that she couldn't get much momentum, but she swung back as hard as she could, feeling the tips of the keys jab into the man's stomach. His grip on her neck loosened, and Monica twisted away from him while stomping back toward his ankle. He stumbled, and she took advantage of the moment to yank her neck free from his grip and lurch forward.

Her balance was off and she was dizzy, but she still managed to stagger away and dart through the swinging door to the living room. She grabbed a nearby chair and flung it to the ground behind her. Continuing on, she grabbed at a lamp and threw it down, and then a small end table, desperate to create obstacles for the creep pursuing her so she could get away.

She fumbled with the old-school latch on the front door before flinging it open and feeling a rush of cold, damp air that snapped her senses into focus.

She'd had no idea it was raining, but after the heat of the fire in the kitchen, she happily sprinted into the chilly, steadily falling drops. Her car wasn't far away. It was parked inside the doorless shed. Her phone was back in the cabin, but she still had the fob for her sedan.

Afraid to look back in case the attacker was gaining on her, she focused on getting to the car.

She'd start it up, back out as fast as she could, and head down the long driveway through the woods to the main road. She steeled herself to run over the attacker if he tried to stop her. He was determined to kill her. She had no choice.

She was nearly to the shed when a lanky figure appeared out of the shadows in front of her and then began to move toward her. This man didn't have a mask. His knitted cap was pulled down low and his collar flipped up so that most of his face was hidden. But she was able to see the broad, mocking smile on his face.

Her steps staggered as she tried to think which way she should go. A dark feeling of fear and hopelessness edged into her consciousness. Her steps faltered. She was exhausted.

Maybe trying to escape was pointless. Maybe the fatal attack on her was inevitable.

No. It's not. She'd made it through so much already. She would not give up now.

The slight nudge of encouragement wasn't a lot, but maybe it was enough to keep her alive.

The only plan she could form was to run into the woods. Were there neighbors nearby who might help? She couldn't remember.

But if she got into the surrounding forest, hunkered down, and stayed absolutely silent, maybe the thugs wouldn't find her. Maybe they would eventually give up and leave.

Or maybe they were excellent trackers who would locate her immediately.

Either way, some part of her had apparently made the decision to give it a try, because she was already running past pine boughs heavy with raindrops at the edge of the long driveway, ignoring the sting as the needles slapped across her face. She tried not to think about the probability that the broken branches would lead the assailants directly to her.

Officer Kris Volker sped down the highway at shortly before four in the morning. While he was not officially on duty, his residence was close to the fire that had been called in by someone living higher up on the mountainside after they'd looked out their window and seen flames at the old Bennett cabin. Kris had gotten the call to respond.

After waking his parents to let them know he was leaving and asking them to make sure his son got to his kindergarten class on time, Kris had hustled out the door to his pickup truck and headed for the two-lane rural highway.

Rain fell at a steady pace, which would hopefully help to contain the flames. Fire and medical emergency crews had been dispatched, but Kris would likely arrive on scene first.

The Bennett cabin had been unoccupied for

several months since Ernest, the eldest member of the clan, passed away. Kris wasn't aware of anyone having taken up residence at the old family homestead since then, but maybe they had. Or perhaps a transient had moved in. In any event, if the cabin wasn't fully engulfed in flames, Kris would do his best to search for anyone who might be inside until the firefighters arrived to take over. His thoughts raced as he pictured the layout of the cabin he'd visited countless times as a kid.

He slowed down for the sharp turn onto the winding drive up to the cabin. As he rounded the first curve, his headlights illuminated a flash of something in the woods that didn't belong there. Jeans and a bright blue shirt. A person running. A woman.

Someone who'd set the fire, intentionally or accidentally, and was now running away?

He hit the brakes. His gut instinct was to go after her. Hold her accountable if she'd burned up the cabin.

But what if there was someone still in the old building? Asleep or unconscious. He had to check on that first. He began to move forward again.

At the end of the final straight section of the drive, he saw a faint orange glow shining on the trees at the back of the cabin. It looked like the rain was doing a decent job of controlling the fire. Also, while still some distance away, he spotted an SUV. The hatch was open, the interior was lit, and two men were grabbing long guns. One of the men also shoved a handgun into his waistband. A thick layer of mud had been smeared across the license plate, making it unreadable.

Something was *very* wrong here.

Kris stopped and killed his headlights.

After thinking for a moment, he decided to move forward and then switch on the high beams, temporarily blinding the men and taking advantage of their disorientation to assert control of the situation. But in the moment between making his decision and taking action, he heard one of the men call out to the other, "Go ahead and shoot her if you have to. We can't let her get away." And then they took off jogging into the woods.

Kris glanced at the burning cabin. He didn't know if anyone was in there. He *did* know a woman was running in the forest while these two creeps intended to go after her and kill her.

He knew what he needed to do.

He backed up his rig until he was closer to the spot where he'd seen the woman. Then he grabbed his radio. "Dispatch, Patrol Eighteen. Advise responders to fire at the old Bennett place that at least two armed gunmen are on scene. I'm checking on female last seen running in the woods. Responders need to use extreme caution on arrival."

"Patrol Eighteen, copy," the dispatcher responded.

Kris turned off the volume on the radio so the bad guys wouldn't hear it.

He got out of the truck, heading in the general direction that he'd seen the woman running, and making adjustments once he spotted snapped branches and twigs and knew he was on her trail.

It appeared she was headed at an angle that would take her to the highway. No doubt when the shadowy men with the rifles picked up her trail—and Kris had little doubt they would, it was that obvious—they would likewise figure out her goal. And they would make sure they were waiting when she got there.

Right now, the potential killers were still behind him and the woman. Kris just needed to find her and help her hide in the darkness without getting tracked and killed himself.

Due to the thick tree canopy overhead, the ground wasn't particularly muddy despite the rain, which helped prevent him from getting bogged down. He spotted pine needles on the ground that formed a low ridge, as if the woman might have begun dragging her feet. Maybe she was injured. Or becoming exhausted.

He sped up and saw her.

For a split second it looked as if she'd seen him. He didn't dare call out since he had no idea how close the gunmen were. He slowed for a second and glanced back but didn't see anyone. When he looked forward again, the woman was gone.

Desperate to catch up with her before she got killed, he pumped his legs harder. As he rounded a thick tree trunk, he felt a branch jut out in his way, causing him to lose his footing. As he fought to right himself, a branch came down hard on the back of his head.

Or maybe it was the barrel of a rifle that had struck him. Somehow the gunmen must have gotten ahead of him.

He thrust his hands forward and managed to catch himself before landing face-first on the forest floor. Then he quickly spun and grabbed at the object that had struck him and yanked it to the side, intending to throw the attacker off balance. It worked.

Somebody stumbled forward and nearly fell on top of him. But it wasn't one of the gunmen. It was the woman.

"It's okay," Kris called out, holding up his arms to fend off blows as she furiously swung the branch at him. "I'm a cop," he called out, trying not to be too loud. The tussle was already making plenty of noise to let the bad guys know where they were, and he didn't want to add to it.

She kept fighting him. He could see the panic in her eyes. He wasn't in his police uniform, and she probably didn't even understand what he was saying.

Obviously the last thing this woman needed at this moment was to be manhandled, but he had no choice. The skin on his back was already itchy as he anticipated a shot coming from one of the attackers any second.

He grabbed both of her hands, and winced when she kicked him in the knee.

"Enough," he said, shaking her hands to try and snap her out of her panic. He knew the visceral feeling of just wanting to stay alive. He'd experienced it himself during a couple of tours overseas in the army. Climbing back down from that height of emotion wasn't an easy thing.

Finally, her gaze focused in a way that told him he had her attention. That she might actually understand him when he spoke.

"I'm a cop with the Cedar Lodge Police Department," he said. "My name's Kris." He quickly explained that he'd gotten the call to respond to the cabin fire and how he'd spotted her running into the woods and then heard the gunmen planning to kill her.

"Great," she said when he finished, breathing heavily, her stance unsteady. She gestured in the direction of the cabin. "Go shoot them."

"I can't."

"Why not?"

For a lot of reasons. He shook his head. "I called for backup to deal with the thugs. Other cops will arrive any minute. I don't want to accidentally shoot one of the responders."

"Oh." She looked around and then picked up the branch she'd used to attack him. "So what do we do now?"

"Wait here until the cavalry arrives." Heading back to his vehicle was too much of a risk. Right now he needed to listen for sounds that the assailants had heard his run-in with the woman and located them. Maybe the patter of rainfall had helped muffle the noise they'd made. But it could also mask the footsteps of the assailants approaching them.

He knelt down to make himself less visible if the criminals were nearby and gestured at the woman to do the same.

"Who are those two men?" he asked in a barely audible whisper. "Why do they want to kill you?"

"I don't know."

Of course you'd say that. Kris didn't want to be a cynic, but sometimes he was one. In his line of work, he'd come across plenty of "nice" people who weren't so nice. People posing as hapless victims when they were anything but that.

There were many more times, though, when people were targeted and attacked who had done absolutely nothing wrong. Maybe he was being played for a fool, but right now he would give this woman the benefit of the doubt.

Bang!

The shot went wild and was followed by several more, some of them smacking the trees and sending splinters of bark and chunks of branch and needles and even pine cones flying.

"They've found us," the woman said in a hoarse whisper. She got to her feet, poised to run. She was still holding the branch to use as a weapon.

Kris shook his head, reached for her free hand and tugged until she squatted back beside him. "If they'd spotted us, they would have snuck up and shot us point-blank. They're trying to panic you and get you to run and show them where you are." He reached for his service weapon, just in case the thugs did pinpoint them. His heart hammered in his chest as he listened for sirens or vehicle engines or any sign of the responders arriving. After a moment, he finally heard something. A high-pitched wail from an approaching patrol car.

With his attention focused in the direction of the siren, he wasn't looking when one of the assailants nearly tripped over them. The thug grabbed the handgun from his own waistband and aimed it at the woman. But then the creep's attention snagged on Kris, and for a moment the shooter hesitated, apparently surprised by seeing an unexpected person.

The woman swung her tree branch and smacked the gunman in the face.

Kris took advantage of the shooter's unsteady steps to grab the woman's arm, shove her behind him, and then back toward the driveway and the arriving cops while pointing his gun in the direction of the attacker.

The gunman and his partner obviously heard the sirens. "You can try to hide but we'll find you!" one of them yelled before firing a couple more shots and then disappearing into the darkness of the forest.

Moments later Kris heard a vehicle start up, and the assailants' SUV tore down the long driveway and turned onto the highway. He keyed his radio and gave the best description he could of the fleeing criminals, their vehicle, and the direction they had gone. "Couldn't get a license plate number," he added.

"Huh," the woman said after his radio communication ended. The two of them continued walking toward the driveway and the flashing red and blue lights visible between the trees.

Not exactly a word, but Kris recognized the feeling of relief she'd expressed.

He thought about the threat voiced by the shooter. For the moment, it made sense for the woman to feel relief. But in the long run, it was apparent that she was still very much in danger. And Kris intended to find out exactly what was going on.

TWO

Monica forced her leaden legs forward as she trudged alongside Kris toward the arriving cops and emergency medical responders positioned at the lower end of the driveway. The fire trucks had already lumbered past, their engines growling as they headed up the graveled driveway on their way to the cabin to fight the flames.

The rain had stopped, the sky was starting to clear, and there was growing light from the oncoming sunrise.

"What's your name?" Kris asked her as they walked.

"Monica."

"Are you injured?"

She was worn out, scratched up from the race through the woods, and it felt like most of her muscles were on fire. But given all she'd been through, none of that seemed particularly dire. In truth, she was grateful to be alive. "I'm all right."

Moments ago she'd overheard him on his radio

requesting the ambulance to stage near the bottom of the driveway with the police cars.

"Are *you* hurt?" She turned to him, realizing that she hadn't given his safety a single thought. He could have been struck by one of the bullets that were flying by while they were under attack.

They cleared the woods and stepped onto the driveway, where she could see him better. He had a sharp jawline, dark brown hair with a hint of rust to it worn in a military-style cut, and icy blue eyes.

"I'm fine," he responded.

He looked like a guy who would typically say that no matter what.

A paramedic hustled toward them. "What's the word?" he asked, giving both Monica and Kris a worried once-over. "Anybody shot? Stabbed? Were you in the burning building and breathed in smoke?"

"Cole, you have an overactive imagination," Kris said.

"Yeah, well, sometimes it saves lives." The medic, a guy with slightly more trendy-looking hair than Kris, turned to Monica. "How are you, ma'am?"

"I'm fine."

"How about we do a quick assessment, just to make sure?"

"*No.*" Her response came out more sharply

than she'd intended, so she added, "Thank you," to soften it.

"You sure? I'm already here, and it wouldn't take long."

"I'm sure."

The medic gave her a hesitant nod before walking away.

Monica's thoughts were starting to race. How could she get this situation wrapped up with the least amount of fuss so she could maintain her low profile?

She couldn't. Not with shots fired at her *and a cop* and the cabin being set on fire.

Kris threw her a suspicious glance.

She didn't blame him. She was full of suspicions, too. And that included suspicion of the integrity of people in the justice system, like the prison guard who had allowed someone to attack her father while he was in custody so he could be sent to solitary confinement at an especially opportune moment for the crime syndicate. Or the person in the prosecutor's office who repeatedly blocked her dad's attempts to offer expanded information about Boyd Sierra Associates—an innocuous name for a very dangerous organized crime group—in return for a reduction in his prison sentence.

Monica dropped her gaze to the ground and absently reached up to rub the stitches on her head. If only she could remember that meeting with her dad before the car crash, she could just do whatever she needed to do and leave town. Despite what the police reports said, she wasn't convinced it had really been an *accident*.

The night before it happened, Monica had told her mom about her father Hunter's claim that Archer worked for the mob, and Suzanne had dismissed the idea out of hand. Monica hadn't realized that Archer had been eavesdropping beyond an open doorway. When Suzanne stepped out of the room to check on dinner, Archer had extended his threat to Monica in a voice so soft and silken that it had turned her blood ice-cold. "You don't know what you're getting into," he'd said quietly. "We have a long reach. We can get to your dad in prison, to you no matter where you go, and to anybody else in your family if that's what it takes to keep control of the situation. It would be better for you if you just let it all go."

"Why are you doing this?" she'd asked.

"Mainly because I love your mother and I want us to be married."

That moment had been the scariest one of all. Because Monica realized that this seriously messed-up individual really did believe his willingness to do anything to possess her mom truly was the definition of love.

And then there was his use of the word *mainly*. What other reasons did he have? Not honorable ones, Monica was certain of that. It probably also had something to do with making sure that the crime syndicate's secrets were indeed kept secret.

She'd known then that she had to get her mom away from Archer and she had to keep her family from getting sucked in further with his criminal associates.

Whether she would ever be able to completely forgive her dad for all the grief and danger he'd brought down on them, she still didn't know.

For seemingly the thousandth time she tried to remember what he'd told her about Cedar Lodge. The small Montana town where her dad had lived when he was young, and where Monica and her parents had come for ski vacations when she was growing up.

Based on the brief voice memo she'd found on her phone, she only knew that Cedar Lodge was important, and she assumed her dad had left something there. Maybe she was wrong, but it was the only place she knew to start. She didn't know what she was looking for, but she'd planned to begin by speaking with people and visiting places connected to her dad.

She'd suspected Archer and the crime group might figure out a way to track her even though she'd kept her specific plans hidden from her mom and only shared them with the two people she'd needed to help her. One of them being her old friend Shelly, who had provided the cabin. Which was now damaged by fire. Monica shook her head slightly. Somehow she would find a way to compensate her for that. But it might take a while to come up with the money.

"So what's the story here, Monica?" Kris asked, sounding and looking very cop-like. "Who are the two attackers, and why did they come after you?"

Before she could answer, a county sheriff's patrol car pulled onto the drive. A dark-haired deputy quickly got out and strode over to them. "Your shooters got away. A couple of us drove a few miles in each direction on the highway, but your assailants must have turned off onto one of the intersecting roads or old logging trails. Or it could be they've just pulled up somewhere close by and are staying out of sight. We'll keep patrol units in the area and continue looking, but for now we've got nothing."

Kris sighed heavily. "Thanks, Dylan. Keep me posted of any updates."

"You sure there were only the two perps and the one vehicle?" the deputy asked, throwing a glance toward the surrounding forest and the thick pines that were becoming more clearly visible with the brightening sunrise.

There could be more. Feeling queasy at the idea, Monica looked around.

"*Could* there be more?" Kris asked Monica with a lifted brow.

She shrugged and wrapped her arms across her midsection. "I don't know. I was asleep. A noise woke me up. I went into the kitchen and it was already on fire. A man attacked me. I got outside, where another man came after me, so I ran into the woods. That's it. That's all I know about any of this."

Kris's radio crackled to life with a report from the captain of the fire crew up at the cabin. "Fire is extinguished. Moderate damage to the kitchen and dining area. Did a search as soon as we arrived on scene. There was no one inside."

"Moderate damage," Kris repeated with a glance at Monica after acknowledging the communication.

"I didn't start the fire," she said. "And now that it's out, I need to go up there and get my belongings." She started walking toward the cabin.

Kris kept pace alongside her. "So, how'd you end up at the old Bennett place?"

Monica wanted to help the police catch the bad guys, but at the same time, it would be like walking a tightrope as she carefully chose what she wanted to say so the authorities wouldn't be alerted to the real reason she was here and then get in her way.

Clearly, in their investigation of what had happened tonight, they would be suspicious of her. She would hope and pray that Kris and his law enforcement friends wouldn't go so far as to surveil her or come along behind her and ask questions of anyone she spoke to. She would also hope and pray that none of the cops or judges in town had connections with the Boyd Sierra criminal group. Like Archer had said in his threat, the association had a long reach.

"My friend Shelly inherited this place from her great-grandpa a few months ago."

"I haven't seen Shelly in ages."

Monica turned to him. "You know her?"

"My family's ranch is just up the road. Our families have been neighbors for generations. How do *you* know Shelly?"

"We met when we were teenagers. Been friends ever since." Monica was aware that this seemingly friendly conversation was actually a subtle interrogation by the cop.

"If you don't know who the attackers were, who do you *think* they might be? What's your best guess on their motive for all of this?"

She shook her head. "I don't know." It wasn't a complete lie. She had no idea who those two creeps were, and she couldn't be certain if this was related to Archer's determination to marry her mom or if some other faction of Boyd Sierra had targeted her, perhaps as a means of scaring her dad into keeping his mouth shut about whatever information he still held regarding their criminal exploits.

They approached the cabin, where a gradually dissipating haze of smoke floated in the air. The kitchen was in the back of the cabin so from the front the building looked mostly okay. She just needed to go inside, grab her stuff, get into the used car she'd bought with the last of her savings after the crash, and go somewhere nearby where she could sit alone and think.

She was scheduled to meet with Esmeralda, an old family friend, at the woman's thrift store in a few hours, and she was determined to keep that appointment. The sooner she got started on what she'd come to Cedar Lodge to do, the better. The last year had taught her that the only way to get out of difficult situations was to go *through* them. Trying to avoid them just made it worse.

"We clear to enter?" Kris asked the fire captain at the front door of the cabin.

"Sure. The power is shut off until an inspector gives the okay to turn it back on. The fire damage messed with some of the wiring."

They walked inside.

Water puddled on the kitchen floor, and droplets fell from the ceiling. The dining table where the fire had started was a pile of soaked, charred wood emitting a strong scorched smell. The window behind it had no glass left in it, and the nearby wall was damaged. In a couple of spots, it had been completely burned through, leaving an irregular hole in its place. Faint sunlight shone into the room.

Monica looked around for her phone. She found it wedged beneath the refrigerator on the side facing away from the fire. It was damp and the screen was cracked, but it had a connection. "It still works," she said in surprise, wiping it with the hem of her shirt.

"We have some extra chargers at the station if you need one."

She turned to him. "I don't want to go to the police station. I have things to take care of today, including calling Shelly and telling her what happened to her cabin." Monica glanced around before retuning her gaze to him. He was handsome. There was no denying that. The brighter light as the sun rose and the clouds rolled away made that quite clear. But what did that have to do with anything? She shook her head slightly, determined to dismiss the observation. "I'd rather just give you my statement here. You already know most of what happened. You were there for it."

He gave her an assessing look that lingered long enough to make her uncomfortable. "Let's talk to the chief together," he finally said in a tone that was light but also left no room for argument. "Maybe having to retell your story from the beginning will help you remember more details."

If she protested too strongly, it would only fuel his curiosity and inflame his suspicion that she was involved in something illegal. The last thing she wanted was a nosy cop keeping an eye on her while she was in town.

"Let me grab my things from the bedroom and put them in my car. I'll follow you to the police station."

"I'll drive you," he said with polite stubbornness. "Afterward, I'll bring you back to get your car. Or drop you off somewhere else if you'd like."

The man's determination was frustrating. But at the same time, she was a little bit grateful despite her annoyance. As she looked around the damaged kitchen, and then walked back to the bedroom to retrieve her belongings, images of the attack flashed in her mind, and fear struck the center of her chest like she'd been punched. She sat on the edge of the bed to steady her breath and regain control of her shaking knees and churning stomach. Since her dad was arrested and her life fell apart, she'd spent a lot of time trying to maintain control of her emotions while dealing with the practical challenges at hand. It never got easy.

It wasn't just the feelings from this attack that were fighting for her attention right now, but also the emotional fallout from the entire last year. Processing all of that was going to take time. Lots more time. Maybe the rest of her life.

She straightened her spine, took a deep breath, wiped her eyes, and got to her feet. Then she grabbed her purse, the backpack stuffed with clothes, and her haphazardly rolled up sleeping bag. At least while riding to the station with Kris she'd feel safe for a while. But she reminded herself not to get used to the feeling of being protected. She still had dangerous work to do.

"So, Monica, what brought you to Cedar Lodge?" Kris asked once they were in his truck and headed down the driveway toward the road.

The young woman beside him kept fiddling with her wavy ash-blond hair, constantly tucking it behind her ears or brushing it from her forehead. When she wasn't doing that, she was adjusting the short necklace she wore or crossing and uncrossing her arms.

She was agitated because she was traumatized after nearly being murdered. He understood that.

He was fairly unsettled himself. But there was something beyond that bothering her, and he was determined to find out what it was. He wasn't going to badger her, though. He wanted her to *want* to talk to him. That was how he preferred to do things whenever possible.

"So, I noticed Nevada plates on your car," he ventured when she didn't reply after a few moments. "You up here in Montana to check out the scenery?"

"My dad is Hunter Larson." The words burst out of her as if the pressure of holding them back had become too much. That name meant nothing to Kris, but he knew better than to interrupt her before she was finished speaking. "He grew up in Cedar Lodge. We used to come on ski vacations. He's a convicted mob accountant who worked for the Boyd Sierra crime syndicate, and this attack probably has something to do with that. I don't know."

The trial and resultant publicity must have been centered down in Nevada, because this wasn't something Kris had heard about. He was, however, aware of the existence of the dangerous Boyd Sierra syndicate.

"But *I* haven't done anything wrong or broken any laws," she added emphatically.

She was fighting back tears. He could hear it in her voice.

He felt sorry for her, but at least now they were getting somewhere. While he wanted to be compassionate, his ultimate goal was to capture the shooters, and he needed as much information as possible to do that.

But organized crime? That wasn't something they had in Cedar Lodge. Unless it happened so efficiently that local law enforcement didn't know anything about it.

The possibility of that sent a chill through him. He'd stayed in Cedar Lodge and lived on the ranch with his parents and son after his wife died in part because he wanted his boy to grow up in a safe town. In fact, he wanted everybody he knew and loved here in Cedar Lodge to live in a safe town. Despite a few inevitable problems, he'd thought that Cedar Lodge had mostly remained untouched by large-scale thug operations like the Boyd Sierra crew. Maybe he'd been wrong.

Organized crime. If the early-morning attackers were professionals, then they might have taken note of his truck as they'd made their getaway. And they weren't likely to give up easily. If they didn't carry through on the directives they'd been given, their employers would be unhappy, and their own lives would be in danger.

For that reason, they likely hadn't fled very

far. It's possible they were actually watching Kris and Monica leave the cabin property right now.

Kris repeatedly checked the truck's mirrors—watching for a tail—as they drove into town. At the police department, he took a lingering look around the parking lot and adjacent streets before they climbed out and he escorted her inside to the chief's office.

Chief Gerald Ellis had a pink box full of doughnuts and a coffeepot brewing on a side table in his office. After offering a greeting and then doughnuts and coffee, he sat in his desk chair, and Kris and Monica sat in front of him.

Kris began with the information Monica had just given him about her father. The chief raised his eyebrows slightly at the mention of the criminal group known for everything from extortion to blackmail to drug trafficking in several Western states.

"I've already received reports from the fire department, sheriff's deputies, and other town cops who were on scene. Now, how about you tell me what happened?" His gaze was on Monica.

She took a small bite of doughnut followed by a couple of sips of coffee and then began her story, starting with hearing a noise in the kitchen and ending with the shooters disappearing into the forest. Even for a former solider with combat experience, it was a nightmarish scenario for Kris to imagine as he listened. He admired her courage and ability to keep a cool head through the ordeal.

"How do you think they found you here in Cedar Lodge?" the chief asked. "And why come after you now?"

Monica shrugged. "Maybe they've been keeping an eye on me for a while. And maybe staying alone in a cabin gave them their first good opportunity to come after me."

Kris didn't think she was lying, exactly, but he still sensed she was holding something back. "I could understand a kidnapping attempt to somehow use you as leverage to control your dad. But this wasn't strictly a kidnapping attempt. It was pretty clear they were willing to *kill* you. Why?"

She reached up yet again to tuck her hair behind her ears. "Maybe they wanted to make my dad fear for my mom's life if he talked too much about the syndicate. Make him afraid that they'd kill her like they killed me if he didn't keep his mouth shut. My mom demanded a divorce after my dad was arrested. But he still cares about her. He hasn't made that a secret."

"Why'd you come to Cedar Lodge?" the chief prompted.

"My dad grew up here. He and my grandparents eventually moved away to Reno. That's where I live. But Dad and Mom and I and sometimes family friends or relatives came up here for a ski weekend every year. We usually came in the summer, too, and sometimes just for an easy vacation. It's how I met Shelly Bennett." She offered a half shrug. "A few days ago, I realized I needed to get away and take a break from everything. Cedar Lodge seemed like a good place for that." She made a sound halfway between a laugh and a sob. "Obviously it was a bad idea."

"I imagine you're anxious to get back to Reno after what's happened." Kris was determined to learn her immediate plans.

She gave a noncommittal shrug.

Sometimes people held back information because they'd done something wrong. But other times it was because they were afraid. Kris thought that might be the situation here. That Monica was afraid to tell them the entire truth.

Chief Ellis leaned back in his chair. "Searching for the thugs will be our top priority. Officer Volker will put together some mug shots for you to look at on the chance the shooters were hired locally. How can we contact you?"

Monica rattled off her phone number, and Ellis typed it into his report form. "Is there anything else you need from me?" Monica asked. "Otherwise, I'd like to get going."

The chief nodded. "That's it for now."

The drive back to the cabin was quiet. Kris gave Monica time to think, hoping she would talk more, but she didn't. Meanwhile, he paid close attention to their surroundings and to other vehicles on the road in case the assailants decided to make another attempt on Monica's life.

When they reached the cabin property, he parked his truck near the shed where Monica had left her car. He exited the vehicle when she did. "I'm happy to take you anywhere you need to go in town," he offered. "Or the county airport if you've changed your mind and want to get out of here in a hurry. Which might be the best idea. You can take care of your car later."

She sighed and ran her fingers through her hair, dislodging a couple of pine needles that had been hidden in there. "I'll be okay."

She glanced toward the cabin, her gaze lingering.

"Whatever is going on, let me help you," Kris said.

She turned to him with a defiant look in her eyes. After a moment it eased into an expression of resolution. "If you want to help, find the shooters who tried to kill the both of us and lock them up."

It was a reasonable response.

"Thank you," she added in a softer tone while

standing by the open door of her car. "I sincerely appreciate all you've done. And I'm beyond grateful that you put your life in danger to help me. But I can take care of myself from here."

A crow shot out of the woods, and she startled.

She was obviously still terrified and on edge after the morning's ordeal. But she'd made it clear she didn't want Kris staying physically beside her, and he needed to respect her wishes.

She started up her vehicle and began down the driveway.

Kris was behind her until they got to the highway and she turned right, toward town. It took some effort to make himself turn left, toward the Double V Ranch, but he did.

He was scheduled to work a patrol shift later today, but first he needed to get back home to make sure his son had gotten to school okay. Then he would saddle up a horse and gather a couple dogs to join him and ride back to the Bennett property as well as the nearby unpaved lanes and fire access roads and homes of the neighbors to see if the bad guys were hiding anywhere around there. The dogs would alert him if there was someone lurking nearby that he didn't see while he conducted his search.

He took one last glance in his rearview mirror before the taillights on Monica's car disappeared from view. An attack like the one this morning in Cedar Lodge was way out of the ordinary. The gunmen had been relentless.

Monica Larson was obviously a smart, tough, and resourceful woman. But Kris still wasn't convinced that she would be all right on her own. He intended to stick very closely to this case because he was certain Monica was still in danger.

THREE

"I'm not sure helping me is the best decision for you," Monica said to the stoop-shouldered woman in front of her. "You might want to change your mind about letting me work here."

"Change my mind?" Esmeralda Marino asked with the arch of an eyebrow while leaning more heavily on her walking cane. "Now, why would I want to do that?"

They were standing inside Esmeralda's store, Start Again Thrift, near the entrance. It was a few minutes past ten, shortly after the store had opened. A young man stood at the register nearby. Monica gestured toward the other side of the store. "Let's head over there." She wanted to explain today's early-morning attack without anyone listening in.

The two women walked until they were surrounded by neatly arranged racks holding blouses and pullover sweaters and there was no one nearby. "All right," Esmeralda said with a stubborn expression on her face—though compassion still showed in her eyes through the thick lenses of her glasses. "Tell me why I would want to change my mind about helping you."

Monica described the attack.

In the hours since parting ways with Kris, she'd done a lot of praying and thinking while sipping coffee and nibbling at the cheap breakfast sandwich she'd bought at a fast-food restaurant. She'd used the restaurant's restroom to change clothes. The jeans and shirt she'd worn during the attack smelled of smoke and were covered with dirt and mud and bits of forest debris from that terrifying chase. The fresher clothes dug out of her backpack smelled faintly of smoke, too, but they were an improvement.

Monica had originally met Esmeralda through a church activity back when she was a teenager and the older lady was a volunteer and Sunday school teacher. Nominally a Christian, Monica had only gone to the advertised teen event because she'd been in town for a few days and she was bored and hoping to make friends. She did make friends, including Shelly Bennett and Esmeralda. And unbeknownst to Monica, she'd taken the first step toward a faith that would help fill the empty spaces in her heart.

Esmeralda had known Monica's dad since he was a kid who played with some of the children in Esmeralda's own family. She also knew several of his childhood friends. It was Monica's hope that Esmeralda would be aware of places in and around town that were meaningful to Monica's dad. Locations where he may have hidden something. Esmeralda had agreed to do her best to help, but now Monica was fearful of putting her friend in danger.

And while she needed the modest sum Esmeralda had offered to pay her for working at the shop for a few days—the teaching career Monica had prepared for had spiraled out of reach when her dad was arrested and then convicted, and her funds were low—she'd figure out some other way to get by while she was in Cedar Lodge if she had to. Maybe sell her car for whatever small amount she could get out of it.

By the time Monica finished her description of the attack, Esmeralda was firmly shaking her head. "Child, if you think I'll turn you away in your time of need, you don't know me at all."

"Things have changed. It's a potentially deadly situation now."

"And you think helping people escape abuse and addiction through our church outreach programs doesn't throw potential danger my way?" Esmeralda scoffed and tapped her cane a couple of times. "I'm not a foolhardy person. But

I'm not going to turn my back on someone who needs my help. Do you really believe I would?"

"No, ma'am. I suppose I don't." Given what Monica had been through, Esmeralda's expression of tough love felt like a hug. The woman's faith and courage and determination to do the right thing made her feel similarly strengthened. And strength was something she would need in abundance.

"Good. Now, I've got a house trailer behind the store that was donated to us. We use the kitchen area of it as an employee break room and the rest of the space for storage when we need to. You can stay there for as long as you'd like."

Monica's eyes welled up with tears. She was filled with gratitude for the reminder that there were still generous and kind people in the world despite the evil that she'd recently witnessed.

Esmeralda led the way outside to the trailer. On the way, they stopped so Monica could grab her backpack out of her car. She had suitcases in the trunk with more clothes, but she could get those later. As they walked, Monica couldn't resist looking around. It seemed unlikely that the assailants would jump out at her behind the thrift store, but then, so many things that seemed unlikely had happened to her over the last year. She did her best to appear calm and collected even if she didn't exactly feel that way.

"Why don't you stay here and rest for a while?" Esmeralda suggested as she opened the trailer door.

Monica stepped inside and set her backpack on a chair beside a table in the compact dining area. The kitchen appliances and furniture looked dated, but it was tidy and had a faint, clean, lemony scent. Maybe staying in town with stores and people nearby would help keep her safe. A wave of goose bumps rippled across her skin as an image of herself struggling with the thickset attacker in the burning kitchen at the cabin popped into her mind. She did her best to push back the fear. She needed to stay in Cedar Lodge and learn what she could to help protect her family. And she'd have to do it despite being afraid.

"I've already done a lot of sitting around this morning," Monica said after doing a quick walk-through of the trailer. "Right now I'd really like to help out in the store and keep myself busy. Meanwhile, maybe you could suggest a place where Dad might have hidden something, so I can get started looking around and hopefully find something helpful?"

"Have you thought about trying to get permission to search the house and surrounding grounds where your dad grew up?"

"I don't know if that would be worthwhile,"

Monica said doubtfully. "My dad and grandparents moved out of that house a long time ago."

But after she thought about it for a moment it began to seem like an idea worth checking out. Her dad had become nostalgic after his arrest and spent time talking with her about his childhood and the path his life had taken. Maybe he'd returned there for a visit while he was out on bail and before he started his prison sentence. And perhaps while he was there he'd hidden something on the property.

"Do you remember where that house is?" Monica asked. "Since my grandparents moved out of Cedar Lodge before I was even born, I've only been to the house once, when my dad showed it to me and my mom. I remember the house and the setting, but I don't remember exactly where it's located."

"I used to work at the nearby elementary school, but I haven't been in that part of town in ages," Esmeralda said. She rattled off the names of a couple of cross streets. "I don't recall the house's address, but if you go over to that general area, send me pictures, and I can probably direct you to the right house."

In light of the attack this morning, wandering around where she could be spotted by the thugs who'd tried to kill her earlier in the day wasn't exactly an appealing idea. But in actuality, it was what she'd come to town to do. "Thank you."

Monica had traveled here with the idea of looking around at the resort where she and her parents had stayed when they'd visited Cedar Lodge. Now she had two locations to search for information her dad might have hidden about his mob associates—and his former friend Archer Nolan in particular. Both ideas could be dead ends, but having someplace to start gave her a small spark of hope.

Back inside the store, Esmeralda found a broom and dustpan and handed them to Monica. "Start with this. I find it soothing to sweep sometimes. Maybe you will, too. I've also got some sorting and pricing for you to do whenever you're ready." After sharing a hug with Monica, she turned and walked away, her cane tapping loudly on the shiny linoleum floor.

Monica began to sweep, noticing that her hands were a little shaky as she tried to let the physical work burn off some of her nervous tension. She tried yet again to recall what her dad had told her about the information he had on Archer Nolan when she visited him in prison. Unfortunately, her mind was still a blank when it came to that topic.

She switched her focus to the goal she had already planned for her first day in town, which was a visit to Elk Ridge Resort. Her parents had kept a time-share at the mountainside complex, connected to a ski resort, for several years before her dad's arrest. They'd managed to get the exact same condo each time. Her dad claimed it had the perfect view of the surrounding mountain peaks as well as the town of Cedar Lodge below. The possibility that she'd find what she was looking for at the first location she checked out was a long shot, but maybe he *had* left something there. Maybe he'd tucked away printed documents or photos. Or perhaps he'd set aside a flash drive or external hard drive in a hidden spot for when he needed it.

Monica heard footsteps behind her, and her heart leaped into her throat. The first thing her mind went to was that it was one of the assailants coming back to finish the job. She grabbed the broom handle with both hands, lifting it to use it as a weapon as she spun around.

It took her a moment to recognize the dark blue of a police uniform and the face of the man wearing it.

"Sorry, I didn't mean to startle you." Kris stopped out of range of her broom while wearing a pensive, somewhat suspicious expression. "You didn't tell me you had a job in town."

Monica lowered the broom and then brushed the hair out of her eyes, her heart still racing despite the realization that she was not under attack. "I wasn't sure I would still have one after the fire and the shootings at the cabin." She did her best to take a deep, calming breath. "And it's not long-term. I'm just helping out for a few days while I'm in town."

"Why?" He glanced around and then moved toward her. "What's the connection?"

Connection? Did he suspect that she was somehow involved with Boyd Sierra and organized crime? That the attack was related to something illegal that he believed she had been involved in? And that she was in town working some kind of unsavory angle on people?

Insulted, she ignored the question and put forth one of her own. "What are you doing here? Have you been following me?"

"Your car is visible from the street."

Monica gave herself a mental head slap. She should have parked behind the trailer where her vehicle would have been out of view. Not to hide from Kris, but to make it more difficult for the shooters to find her.

"I have some mug shots for you to look at." Kris held out a tablet. "These are local criminals and ex-cons with violent histories. Maybe someone looks familiar. I didn't get a clear look at either of the attackers' faces, so I can't give any input on this."

"I didn't see them clearly, either," Monica said, reaching for the device. "But I'll take a look." She swiped through a couple dozen photos, but none of the images stood out to her. "Sorry," she said, handing the tablet back to Kris. "Nobody looks familiar." Her voice broke on the last word, as it sank in how difficult it might be for the cops to find the assailants. Maybe they wouldn't be able to find the thugs before they attacked her again.

"Try not to be discouraged," Kris said. "This is just a start."

Monica heard the familiar sound of Esmeralda's cane tapping the floor.

"Kris, good to see you," Esmeralda called out, walking up to them.

"Good to see you, too." He smiled at the older lady, and for a moment the expression of cop suspicion on his face was replaced by a sweet, almost boyish, grin. He carried a warm, masculine appeal that would most definitely have attracted Monica's interest if her life circumstances were different. And if he didn't seem so convinced she'd done something wrong.

"So you two know each other," Monica prompted Esmeralda.

"We see each other nearly every Sunday in church." She glanced at Monica with a slight smile on her lips before turning back to Kris.

"Were you the officer who responded to the cabin fire and helped her escape those bad men?"

Kris nodded.

"How about that." Esmeralda shook her head. "Monica first came to our church when she was fifteen years old. I'm surprised you never crossed paths when she was in town and came to services."

An awkward moment passed when it felt like the Sunday school teacher was trying to set them up for a date. Which stirred up a weird mixture of feelings that Monica couldn't even begin to identify. Because she didn't want to. So many things demanded her attention that it didn't really feel like her life was her own anyway. What did it matter if she met an attractive man?

A cashier at the front of the store called out to Esmeralda for assistance.

"You keep this girl safe," Esmeralda said to Kris before walking away.

"I'll be leaving town in a few days," Monica told Kris, trying to send a clear signal that she was not interested in him despite Esmeralda's efforts. She was tired, she was stressed, and she was worried about her parents, both of whom were obviously not so great at making life choices. The last thing she needed to do was stir up any kind of interest she might have in a police officer who apparently thought she was a criminal. At least, his questions made it seem that way.

"I just want to help," Kris said quietly. "Maybe you're being blackmailed. Or it could be you're afraid to speak up about certain information because you fear more attacks. We all make bad decisions sometimes that we regret and that end up causing us trouble. But I'm sure there's a way to make this better."

Was he sincere? Or was he just looking to bust somebody—anybody—to impress his superiors in the police department and help his career? After being told lies by investigators and also witnessing questionable actions in the agencies that were supposed to ensure justice, Monica was determined to be very careful about whom she trusted.

A small voice inside told her Kris might be the real deal. Someone who wanted to do the right thing. Somebody who truly wanted to help her. But right now, she just couldn't take the leap of faith to trust him.

"I'll be fine," she said, turning her attention back to sweeping.

"All right," he said after a moment's hesitation. "But be careful and watch your back."

She listened to him walk away.

After he was gone, she found herself wishing

he had stayed. Because he made her feel safe. And she told herself that there was no other reason.

Five hours later, Monica drove up the steep driveway and past the stone signs announcing the Elk Ridge Resort, a complex that included privately owned homes plus time-share condominiums.

She was exhausted but still determined to start her search. The sooner she got going on this—and any other ideas she could think of—the sooner she'd be able to leave town and end any chance of putting Esmeralda in danger by staying on her property.

Maybe she'd seen too many movies, but it did seem possible she could track down the information her father had hidden.

It was upsetting that her mother had dismissed Monica's warnings about Archer and demanded proof before she would even consider the man was not the upstanding citizen he claimed to be. But Suzanne Larson had never been inclined to deal with uncomfortable situations directly. She'd do nearly anything to avoid them. Even a conversation, if it involved something stressful, was dismissed or circumvented. She liked living in her own world of denial as she enjoyed creature comforts and focused on hosting impressive dinner parties.

While Monica had been shocked by the revelation that her dad worked for organized crime, she wondered if her mom had had an inkling that something out of the ordinary was going on. Maybe, since Suzanne hadn't seen any blatant proof of misbehavior, she'd been able to enjoy the generous amount of money pouring into the household without questioning too closely where it came from or how it had been earned.

Stop it. Monica told herself she was being uncharitable.

Even if her suspicions were true, that didn't dim Monica's drive to protect her mom and potentially the rest of her family—her aunts and uncles and cousins who could end up endangered by an association with organized crime.

She reached up to touch the scar on her head, wishing she could remember what her dad had said to her before the car crash took away that part of her memories. She huffed in frustration. Quickly, her frustration shifted to fear as her thoughts turned back to this morning's attempt on her life. Nearly being shoved into a fire. Being chased in the woods, anticipating the burn of a bullet smacking into her body. She shuddered and glanced in the rearview mirror to see if anyone was following her. At the moment, there was no one there.

Maybe the two shooters actually had left town.

But if that were the case, the mob would likely send two more.

The long driveway rose in elevation, past forest and toward surrounding jagged peaks and the mountaintop. Late-afternoon sunlight deepened the shadows nearby and higher up the mountainside. Cedar Lodge was located in a river valley that often felt cut off from the rest of the world. The fun, relaxing times Monica had spent here in the past felt like they'd happened a lifetime ago.

Like a lot of people before him, Hunter Larson found faith in prison when he hit rock bottom. Suzanne didn't believe it was real, but Monica did, and her father's faith journey forged a new connection between the two of them, motivating her to put her anger and feelings of betrayal aside and to visit him more often. On one visit, she'd asked him why he'd thrown away a good life to work for organized crime.

"Fool's gold," he'd responded with a sad laugh and a shake of his head. "I don't mean that the money they paid me was fake. It was real enough. But the feeling I was chasing—contentment, I suppose, or a sense that I was making the most of my life and impressing other people—never materialized."

He'd been making decent money as an accountant when he was first introduced to a member of Boyd Sierra Associates by a mutual friend and the organization offered him some very well-paying legitimate accounting work. He'd had no idea that he was working for organized crime at the start. Then, slowly, they'd asked him to change a few numbers here and there and create false financial documentation to replace records that had been "lost."

"Of course I figured out what was going on, but it was great having the extra money in return for very little work," he'd told Monica on one visit, crossing his arms over his chest before blowing out a breath and shaking his head. "But slowly, it started to bug me. I knew it was wrong, and it could cause problems for you and your mom and me farther down the road."

He'd cleared his throat, looking thoughtful at that point.

"I wanted out of the organization, so I started talking to them about moving on to other things. They weren't happy to hear about my intentions, but I began making plans to exit anyway. I put things in place so I'd be ready to get out of the operation and stay out. Then one of the association's front companies that I'd helped launder money through went to the authorities and reported that I'd defrauded them. Now here I am in prison. And ultimately it's nobody's fault but mine. I made the stupid, foolish decisions."

Put things in place. Right now those specific words that he'd used swirled around in Monica's head. What *things*? And where was the place?

She pulled up in front of the resort's administrative office and parked.

Inside the office, she spotted a young woman at the reception desk who looked familiar. Hopefully, she'd worked there the last time Monica had come with her family for a visit. If she recognized her, she might be more inclined to help her.

Monica hated to lie, but she didn't want to burden this person with her whole story of dangerous attacks. Especially since it might scare the woman and cause her to turn down Monica's request. So she combined her request to have a look around in their usual condo with a statement that was actually true even if it didn't include the entire story. "I think my dad might have left something behind the last time we were here, and even though it's been a while we only recently realized it. If possible, I'd like to take a quick look around in the condo where we stayed."

"We do thorough cleanings on a regular basis," the receptionist said in a friendly tone. "I think we would have come across it. When that happens, we immediately contact the most recent guest and then ship them the item if they request it."

From her demeanor, Monica got the impression the woman did recognize her from prior trips and either didn't know about Hunter Larson's criminal conviction or didn't hold it against Monica.

"Sometimes things fall into a crack or crevice and they're overlooked," Monica responded with a slight shrug.

The receptionist hesitated for a moment. "Which unit?"

Monica gave her the information.

She'd hoped the woman wouldn't ask specifically what she was looking for—since she didn't know—and was grateful when she didn't.

After a few moments tapping at the screen of the tablet in front of her, the woman looked up. "It's unoccupied right now, so I suppose it wouldn't hurt to take a look."

They headed down one of the narrow lanes in the complex on foot, making their way around a small cement mixer and a truck belonging to a paving company. A man with curly red hair and dirt-covered clothes, carrying a shovel, stepped out from behind the truck and nearly collided with Monica. He muttered an apology and continued on his way.

"We're always doing upkeep," the receptionist said in a chipper tone.

So did that mean if Hunter had left some physical item here, it could have been discovered or disturbed during a routine maintenance project?

They'd walked around the truck when Monica caught the approach of someone from the corner of her eye.

"Hey, look who's back," a man called out.

Monica panicked, thinking he might be another mob gunman putting on a show of friendliness so he could get close enough to kill her. Heart suddenly pounding, she tensed her muscles and got ready to run.

But then she recognized the tall, balding figure of Ryan Fergus. A semiretired former general contractor about twenty years older than Monica's dad, he'd spent time in the Reno area before relocating to Cedar Ridge, where he worked part-time for the resort. He and Monica's dad had hit it off and chatted when her family came to visit.

The knot in her chest shifted from stark fear to dread and apprehension as she waited for the robust older gentleman, who was an affirmed ski bum, to ask about her dad. She really didn't want to talk about all that had happened. For one thing, it still hurt every time she recounted her dad's arrest and imprisonment. And for another, she'd found that, oftentimes, people who inquired about Hunter were hoping for salacious details more than expressing genuine concern.

Beyond that, what if the receptionist overheard their conversation and had second thoughts about letting Monica into the condo?

In the end, Ryan offered a kind smile that reached all the way to his deeply lined eyes and asked, "Monica, how are you?" He reached out for a lingering handshake that gave her the impression he knew about her dad's situation and wanted to be gracious about it.

"I'm well," she replied, anxious to get to the condo and wanting to avoid a full conversation.

"Glad to hear it. My best to your family." He indicated the paving company truck. "I need to get back to supervising some repairs. Hard winters make for good skiing, but they sure do some damage."

He continued on his way, and Monica resumed walking with the receptionist until they reached their destination. The two-story condo had a stylish entrance facing the access road and a modest yard in the back with a patio, a swath of grass, and a white rail fence on the edge of a stony cliff that allowed for a breathtaking view of the entire valley, including the town of Cedar Lodge, down below.

The receptionist settled in the dining area, taking calls for the resort, while indicating to Monica that she was free to look around.

Monica checked hiding places she'd seen on

TV cop shows: the undersides of drawers where an object could be taped, the backs of dressers, atop the ceiling tiles near a couple of larger air vents, and the very backs of top shelves in the closets. She even took a close look at the assortment of hardcovers and paperbacks left on a pair of wall shelves in the living room in case something was hidden inside or behind one of them. She tried tapping the stones around the fireplace to see if one of them might be loose. Nothing.

She went outside to look around the backyard. Despite the cool breeze, sweat beaded on her forehead and between her shoulder blades. She imagined someone in the shadows getting a clear view of her on the edge of the cliff and firing a shot. She might be taking a risk standing out here, but this was what she'd come here to do. People's lives were in the balance, including her own, so she did her best to shake off her feeling of unease and power through.

She searched for anything that appeared out of place. Maybe one of those hollowed-out fake rocks where you could hide a key inside. She walked the fence line, looking at the ground there, and then behind the evergreen hedges, but nothing caught her eye.

Swallowing down the disappointment that had her on the verge of tears, she thanked the receptionist, and they walked back to the admin building, where they parted ways.

She headed back down the mountainside to the highway and then into town. The vehicle she drove was nondescript, but Kris mentioned noticing her out-of-state car plates, and she felt like an easy target. Despite gripping the steering wheel, her arms and hands began to feel shaky.

When she thought of the handsome cop, she forced herself to set aside the mental image of him. She didn't want to let her thoughts linger there. Instead, she considered whether it would be wise to hide her car and use rideshare services to get around town. The problem was that the cost would quickly add up, and her credit cards were nearly maxed out.

Figuring her shakiness might be due not only to fear of being found by the bad guys but also to low blood sugar—she hadn't eaten much today—she stopped at a grocery store on her way back to her temporary trailer residence.

After purchasing a couple of bags' worth of food, she walked back out to her car, drove the few blocks to the thrift store, parked in the grass beside the trailer, and walked up the wooden steps that served as a front porch.

She inserted the key Esmeralda had given her, pushed open the door, and heard an odd clicking sound. At the same moment, she noticed a length of wire across the doorframe that hadn't been there earlier.

Bomb!

Flinging the bags aside, Monica threw herself off the steps.

FOUR

"I'm all right." Monica clasped her hands together and brought them to her chin. "I just need to rest for a few minutes. And I need some time to think."

Kris stood with one hand on the frame of his patrol car, leaning partway through the open door and peering closely at the mysterious woman seated in front of him. Why was Monica Larson so relentlessly targeted for attack? Just being related to a mob accountant didn't seem like reason enough. And why was she determined to remain in Cedar Lodge after all of this violence?

"Really," she said with a shallow nod and a faint, obviously forced smile. "I'm okay."

Kris's concern must have been evident on his face.

"I don't have any broken bones or sprains or burns," she added. "I flattened myself on the grass after I jumped off the steps, and the force of the blast went over me." She unclasped her hands and looked at them. "Just some scrapes." The nervous smile came back. "And grass stains on my clothes."

Kris had heard the call go out over dispatch after a nearby resident phoned 9-1-1 to report the explosion. Esmeralda had already let him know that Monica was staying on the property. He'd been first on scene, heart dropping to his feet when he'd seen the trailer engulfed in flames, certain the attackers had gotten to Monica and killed her.

It had taken him a moment to spot her silhouette outlined by the fire. She'd been curled up on the grass, clearly terrified and afraid to move. He'd gotten her into his patrol unit just as Fire, EMS, and additional cops arrived. While helping her to his vehicle, he'd kept one hand free, ready to grab his gun if necessary. The attackers might have been lingering nearby, ready to finish her off if she hadn't perished in the fire. But there hadn't been an immediate follow-up attack. Perhaps the thugs had hung around but they hadn't expected a cop to respond so quickly.

There were plenty of police and first responders around now as the fire crew finished dousing the flames that had devoured much of Esmeralda's trailer. It looked like Monica would be safe for the moment. But he had no doubt the assailants would try again.

"Tell me what's really going on," Kris said, doing his best to check his frustration so this didn't sound like an interrogation.

"I already did. The mob's trying to get to my dad by harming me."

"That doesn't tell me why you're determined to stay in town. There must be a reason."

She gave a slight shrug in response.

"Don't you want to go home?" Didn't she have family or friends she could turn to for help?

"I can't go home." She glanced through the windshield of the patrol car at the trailer, where a few small flames lapped at the twisted metal frame of a blown-out window. "If I go back to Reno, I might as well just walk straight toward the thugs who are trying to kill me."

Of course he wouldn't ask her to do that. And she apparently didn't have the financial resources to go far away where she couldn't be found and stay there indefinitely.

How could he help her? He'd called Shelly Bennett to confirm that Monica had permission to stay in the cabin. Shelly had already known about the initial attack—Monica had called and told her—and Shelly had asked Kris to do whatever he could to help Monica. She'd said that

Monica was a good friend and a good person. Esmeralda had likewise vouched for Monica.

So why was Kris so wrapped up with worrying about what might happen to this woman?

Maybe it had something to do with the moment he first spotted her in the woods, running for her life. And the moments later, when he'd been beside her as she'd used the only weapon she could reach—a tree branch—to fight to survive. On her own, and desperate. With only him, a stranger, to help her.

Stationed overseas in the army, he'd seen so many people with their lives torn apart, no home and no one to help them as they grimly tried to hang on and keep living for just one more day. Kris had done his job there the best he could while he was in the military, but he'd seen so many people he couldn't help.

And then there'd been his wife Angie's devastating medical diagnosis eighteen months after Roy had been born. Pancreatic cancer. Spreading quickly. Another sorrowful situation where he couldn't do anything.

But right here, right now, he might be able to assist Monica while at the same time capturing some very bad guys. He hoped to uncover the extent to which organized crime was operating in his town and help crush it. Of course, he also wanted to lock up any local criminals who might be working with these dangerous men.

"I'm going to talk to the chief for a minute." Kris beckoned another officer to stay near the patrol car where Monica was still seated until he came back. The chance of the assailants launching the follow-up attack on Monica that he was worried about might be small, but it was not an impossibility.

Cops had already been dispersed to canvass the nearby residential neighborhood as well as the other businesses on Glacier Street in search of witnesses or helpful video footage. Esmeralda had a couple of outside security cameras that had hopefully recorded some useful images.

Chief Ellis was talking to the fire chief when Kris walked up. As soon as the fire cooled down enough to get a closer look, their intention was to learn as much as possible about the explosive device and see what investigative leads they could develop from there.

Cole was also there with his paramedic crew, waiting for the fire to be completely extinguished and the scene to be officially cleared before he left. Cole had prodded Kris to ask Monica one more time if she was certain she didn't want a quick medical checkup just to confirm that she was all right. Which was what Kris had just done.

"What did she say?" the paramedic asked.

"She said she's okay," Kris reported.

Kris, Cole, and Deputy Dylan Ruiz—along with their friend Henry Walsh, who was away overseas right now—had known each other since they were small and had played football together in high school. After graduation they'd all joined various branches of the military. Kris, Cole, and Dylan had returned to Cedar Lodge and taken jobs protecting the citizens of their town while also working on their family ranches. Henry had gone on to work as a hostage rescue specialist for an international private security company. Nobody was ever quite sure where he was or what he was doing. But he did check in every now and then.

"Okay," Cole said thoughtfully. "Encourage her to go to the hospital and get checked out if she develops any concerning symptoms."

Kris nodded. Monica obviously didn't think she needed a medical assessment, but she would need a place where she could rest, knowing that she was safe while she thought things through and decided on her next step. He was afraid the thugs would get to her if she stayed in a hotel in town.

Gazing at the smoldering trailer and considering how close she'd come to death twice in one day, he stepped away from Cole and the police chief. He slid his phone out of his pocket and put through a call to his mom, Jill.

"The woman I told you about who was in the fire at the cabin this morning, Monica, has been attacked again," he said after exchanging quick greetings with his mother. "She needs a place to stay. For tonight, at least. I was thinking we could put her up in the bunkhouse. She'll be away from the main house so she won't be around you or Dad or Roy. I'll throw down a sleeping bag outside the bunkhouse door or maybe a small tent so I can keep an eye on things. She's been through a lot, and she could use a break. Would you be okay with that?"

The bunkhouse had actually been remodeled into a large studio apartment, but they kept the old name. Kris's brother stayed in it whenever he left his job in Alaska to come for a visit.

"Let me talk to your father, and I'll call you right back." Jill disconnected.

Kris's dad, Pete, was a military veteran. His mom had been a competitive barrel racer. Both of them had grown up on ranches on the edge of wilderness, and they'd raised two rambunctious sons who'd gone on to serve in combat zones. Challenges, quickly changing circumstances, and exposure to risk were not unusual or intimidating for Kris's parents.

He was concerned about Roy, though. What if

someone came to the ranch looking for Monica? It might be a good night for Roy to sleep over with his cousins. In fact, it might be wise for him to go for a visit even if Monica didn't stay in the bunkhouse. That attack at the cabin was literally close to home, and the possibility existed that the thugs were hiding in the area. There were plenty of vacation homes that weren't occupied by their owners for much of the year. And there were remote campgrounds not too far away.

Kris threw a glance toward Monica inside the patrol car and the cop standing nearby keeping an eye on her. He saw that everything was okay, and then went for a walk around the perimeter of the thrift store and the surrounding property looking for anyone lurking nearby or possibly evidence left behind. Unfortunately, he didn't spot anything helpful.

He was nearly back to his patrol car when his phone rang. It was Jill.

"Listen, I don't want to put you and Dad in a difficult situation," he started out.

"Don't be silly," Jill cut in before he could continue. "Bring Monica here. And we've told Roy that he's going to be staying with his other grandparents tonight. Just to be safe. Hope you're okay with that."

His mom had been one step ahead of him. Of course.

His late wife's parents, Yvonne and Gabriel Durand, were very involved in Roy's life, and the two families had remained close in the aftermath of Angie's passing.

"That sounds like the perfect arrangement," Kris said, mildly annoyed with himself for not having thought of it first.

"Good. Roy's excited that tomorrow morning, they'll be the ones taking him to school for the first time."

"I imagine he is."

"When do you think you'll get here?"

"Within an hour."

"Okay. I'll have dinner ready for the both of you."

"Mom, you don't need to do that. We can pick up something in town and bring it to the house."

"You think you can get better food in town?" she asked with mock sternness.

"No, ma'am."

"Good. See you in a bit. And watch yourself."

Didn't matter that he was a combat veteran and a cop. His mom still couldn't resist reminding him to be careful.

Kris walked back to where the chief and Cole were still standing.

"I'm going to have Campbell take lead on the full investigation of all of this," Ellis said at Kris's approach. "I'll have him start by contacting the feds for any information they're willing to give us on the Boyd Sierra syndicate. We'll also talk to them about any recent bombings using the same kind of device that's present here."

Sam Campbell was one of three detectives in the police department.

"Meanwhile, I want you to keep an eye on Monica. See what you can learn. And keep her alive, obviously."

"Actually, I've already got a plan to run by you regarding that."

"Let's hear it."

"She still refuses to leave town. Going home to Reno is out of the question. I'm afraid if she checks into a hotel, she might not be alive in the morning."

The chief nodded his agreement so far.

"Unless we have some kind of safe house in town that I don't know about, I think the smartest thing to do is have her stay at the Double V Ranch with my family. At least for tonight."

"You sure you want to expose your family to the danger that could potentially come from that?"

Kris explained the planned arrangement.

As he finished, the chief responded to a call over his radio.

"What's this?" Cole asked Kris in a teasing

tone while the chief was distracted. "A woman has finally piqued your interest?" He smiled broadly.

"It's not like that," Kris snapped. Yes, Monica was pretty. But Cedar Lodge was full of pretty women. Well-intentioned friends and family members had tried to set him up with some of them. But between being a cop, working the ranch, and being a dad—the most important job of all—he didn't have time to date. Angie had specifically told him before she passed that she wanted him to find love again—for Roy's benefit as well as for his own sake. But he still felt like *moving on*, as people termed it, would somehow diminish the love he'd had for his late wife. If he'd really loved her, how could he just *move on*?

Right now none of that mattered. He wasn't offering to help Monica because of a romantic interest. He wanted to help because there was so much suffering in the world. Why not do what you could to ease that for someone? To help keep them from getting *murdered*?

Cole dampened down his smile, but not by much. Not even when Kris glared at him.

Ellis completed his radio conversation and turned his attention back to Kris. "Let's go see what Monica thinks about staying at your family's ranch."

At the patrol car, Kris extended his invitation to Monica.

She shook her head in response. "Thanks, but I've already caused enough trouble. I'll just find a hotel, and I'll lay low for a couple of days."

"I'm not sure you'll last a couple of days," Kris responded.

Her eyes grew wide, and Kris felt a little bad about being so blunt. But not bad enough to backpedal on what he'd said. Because it was the truth.

"You're free to do what you want, of course," the chief said. "But the Double V Ranch would be a good place for you to stay, at least for tonight."

She hesitated for a moment before pressing her lips together and then nodding. "Okay."

"Good," Kris said as he and the chief stepped back from the open door of the patrol car to make room for Monica to get out. He didn't realize until that moment that he'd been holding his breath, waiting for her response. Now he just hoped that the ranch would really be a peaceful place for her to recover from all that had happened to her in one very long day. And that the assailants didn't try to launch another attack tonight.

"I left my groceries flung across the lawn in front of the trailer," Monica said as they neared the edge of town on the way to Kris's ranch. "Can we stop somewhere so I can grab something to eat?"

Despite nearly being blown to bits, Monica was ravenous. She was tired and had a pounding headache, too. But right now she was focused on food.

"My mom's making us something to eat," Kris said. "But we can stop at the burger place and get you something if you'd rather do that."

"I can wait," she said. A home-cooked meal sounded wonderful.

Kris opened the patrol car's console and pulled out a bottled water and a smashed granola bar. "They've been in here awhile," he said apologetically.

"I don't care." Monica accepted both and ripped off the end of the granola bar wrapper. "Thank you," she managed to add before taking a big bite of oatmeal and chocolate.

"Why are you doing this?" she asked after she finished eating and had drunk all the water. "Why are you sticking your neck out this far and letting me stay at your home?"

She tried to be a charitable person and help others in need, and she understood the drive to do that. But a cop who'd met her less than twenty-four hours ago offering her refuge in his home seemed like a lot. She wasn't sure she could do that for someone, let alone for a complete stranger.

"I want to keep you alive, and I'd also like to get to the bottom of these attacks. The Cedar Lodge PD needs to make sure dangerous thugs don't get the impression that they can run roughshod over this town."

Fair enough. She assumed that he would now press her for more information, but he didn't. And she found herself thinking that maybe she actually was ready to tell him everything. That she was staying in town because she was looking for evidence of Boyd Sierra Associates' criminal activity she believed her father had left here. And that she was desperate to convince her mother to break off her engagement to a mobster before they got married in two weeks.

She took a deep breath, pondering her options.

Full night had fallen, and they rode in the darkness without further conversation. They approached the foot of the drive leading to the Bennett cabin, and Monica felt a shiver pass through her as they drove by.

Thank You, Lord.

Her life could have ended this morning. It was a disquieting thought, to say the least. She glanced over at Kris, his features visible in the dashboard light. Would she have survived if he hadn't been there? There was no way to know. But she was grateful for his help.

They turned off the highway onto a winding tree-lined drive that finally opened to a multiple-acre expanse of meadow and stables and corrals and various outbuildings. A rambling ranch house sat at the edge of a circular unpaved turnaround near the front entrance. The Craftsman-style structure had large windows with light spilling out into the darkness, and there were several vehicles parked nearby.

"You and your parents live here?" Monica asked.

"And my son, Roy."

But not Roy's mother? Were she and Kris separated? Divorced?

What difference does it make?

None. It made no difference. Why did she care? She didn't.

Okay, maybe she was a *little* curious about Kris's personal life. Maybe she was a little bit attracted. But it was probably just nerves and fear talking. He'd made her feel safe. That was the appeal. And that was all.

To her surprise, Kris came around and opened the patrol car door for her as she was gathering her backpack and doing what she could to smooth her hair and try to look presentable.

They walked up to the door, and she was feeling

oddly nervous. Like she wanted to make a good impression on his family for some silly reason.

Kris opened the door and ushered her ahead of him. As soon as Kris stepped into the house, he was attacked by a small boy dashing across the living room toward him like a runaway colt.

Monica's gaze locked on the boy and his father as Kris picked up the little guy.

Kris had said his son's name was Roy, and Roy had his dad's features but with dark brown eyes instead of blue and dark brown hair instead of Kris's more russet-brown. The child had chubby, rosy cheeks, and he seemed giddy with excitement.

Monica stood by listening as Roy chattered to his dad about his surprise trip to stay at Grammy Yvonne and Grandpa Gabriel's house.

"This is Monica," Kris said to his son.

The exuberant boy had a sudden attack of bashfulness and buried his face in Kris's neck.

Finally, Monica shyly turned to face the adults. She wasn't certain what kind of reception to expect.

While holding his son in his arms, Kris made the introductions. His mother, Jill, stepped forward first. She was a petite woman with her red hair styled in a pixie cut. A deep tan spoke of time spent working outside. "Welcome," she said to Monica.

His father, Pete, had Kris's muscular build. He, too, offered a friendly "Welcome to our home."

Kris introduced his son's other set of grandparents, and that was when Monica learned that Roy's mother had passed away three years ago.

Kris reported the story in a matter-of-fact tone, but it pierced Monica's heart. This kind man had lost his wife, and this sweet little boy had lost his mother. It was a sorrowful reminder that nearly everyone faced some kind of tragedy in their lifetime.

Maybe it was her own exhaustion combining with compassion for this kind family, or maybe it was a delayed response to the day's terrifying events, but Monica found her eyes were pooling with tears. Embarrassed, she sniffed loudly and turned away to wipe at her eyes with the edge of her sleeve. Then she did her best to pull herself together and politely engage in conversation.

With constant glances at the little boy listening in, and obviously mindful of what they wanted to say in front of him, the grown-ups talked very generally about what had brought Monica here.

After Kris gave his son one last hug and a half dozen more kisses, the little boy excitedly left with his visiting grandparents. Kris stood on the porch, watching until they were out of sight.

"After we eat dinner, I'll get you set up in the bunkhouse," Kris said to Monica. "I'll be sleeping outside the door. And don't worry, it's not as rustic as it sounds. It's pretty nice, really."

"Oh, honey, I already fixed up one of the guest bedrooms for her," Jill said to her son. She turned to Monica. "Shelly Bennett thinks very highly of you." She threw a quick glance at Kris. "You're not the only one who spoke to her today." Her attention reverted back to Monica, and she added, "Shelly asked me to do everything I can to help you. I intend to."

Tears started to well up in Monica's eyes again. So much kindness on the heels of such horror was overwhelming.

Jill offered a sympathetic smile. "I left some chicken enchiladas and rice in the oven for you two." She walked toward the kitchen, a large space with a breakfast nook. Monica and Kris followed. "There's iced tea in the fridge." She glanced at Kris. "Dad and I already ate."

Pete stood near the kitchen entrance.

"We get up early, we eat dinner early, we go to bed early," Jill explained to Monica with a smile. "That's just what ranch life is like. Now we'll leave you two alone to eat and talk in private about police business. We've got security cameras on the property and spoiled dogs who will bark if anyone comes around."

Monica reached down to pet the large hound of indeterminate breed that had been watching her with interest since she'd arrived. A second, apparently shier dog stayed near Kris's dad.

"That gentle giant you're petting is Betty," Pete said. "The little one is Pepper. The other dogs prefer to stay out in the stables with the horses." Betty followed Jill as she walked toward her husband.

After they were gone, Kris opened the oven to pull out a covered dish and set it on the stove top.

Monica glanced around. "How can I help?"

"Why don't you just sit down and relax. This will be ready in a minute."

A short time later, Monica had a plate of delicious-looking food in front of her, along with utensils and tea.

She was just about to close her eyes and offer a silent prayer of thanks when she saw Kris do the same. She wanted to ask him if he was praying, but she didn't feel like she had the right to. He was a public servant helping her stay alive. They weren't friends.

And yet, she already respected and admired him. He was a gentle man, but he was strong, too. He'd followed through on his determination to help her and work on her case without coercing or pressuring her into doing anything she didn't want to do.

After a few moments she realized she'd been gazing at him for a little too long. Fortunately, he hadn't seemed to notice. A warm bloom of embarrassment spread across her cheeks, and she turned her attention to her food.

The enchiladas were savory and delicious. There wasn't much conversation between the two of them, which gave her time to think. After their meal was completed, Monica knew she wanted to tell Kris everything about why she was here and what she was attempting to do. Even though she suspected he would try to stop her from doing it.

He listened attentively while she went through it all, some of it a repetition of what he'd already heard, but she needed to say it again to give her plans context.

"How's your head?" was the first thing he asked, making her laugh in surprise. She reached up to touch the stitches where her scalp had been split in the crash.

"Everything physical is healing okay. The memories? Not so much. I still have some vague impressions I think might be memories, but they vanish as soon as I try to focus on them."

Kris folded his napkin and set it beside his plate. "I understand what you're attempting to do and why," he said in measured tones. "I also think you realize now why you can't do it alone. Staying with you while you carry out your plan might be one way to investigate the attacks against you and track down the criminals while keeping you safe. Detective Campbell will be doing his research-based investigation. Me shadowing you would give us more boots-on-the-ground-type information. It would broaden the scope of the investigation."

A weight lifted off Monica's chest. The last thing she'd expected was that Kris would offer to help her with what she was doing.

"Let's talk to the chief about this in the morning," he added.

They cleared the table, and then Kris showed her the way to her room. Along the way, he grabbed her backpack from the spot near the front door where she'd set it down.

They passed a den where Jill and Pete were watching a movie. Jill got up and came along to help Monica get situated, showing her where she could find towels in the bathroom connected to her room. Betty and Pepper came with her. This time the little black-and-white terrier mix let Monica pet him.

"We'll let you get some rest," Kris said before leaving Monica alone in her room.

Monica flopped down onto the bed and tried to relax. The Volker family were all very nice people, and they had a beautiful home. But there was no escaping the fact that she was here hiding from people who were trying to kill her. And this was just the end of her second day trying to fight back against the mob to protect her parents and herself. It was going to be a dangerous fight, and there was no guarantee she would win.

FIVE

Sitting beside Monica in Chief Ellis's office while waiting for the chief to return from a brief meeting, Kris looked down at his phone and waved at the video chat image of his son. "Love you, buddy."

"Love you, too, Dad." Roy waved back before shoving the phone into his grandma Yvonne's hand and then scampering away.

Yvonne moved the phone until the camera was at face level. Her expression slightly chagrined, she offered a one-shoulder shrug and said, "He just saw his friends."

Yvonne had taken Roy to school this morning, and while Kris understood his son's need to be social, he still couldn't help feeling a little hurt. Which was silly. Ranch life could be isolating for a kiddo with no siblings, and one of the major benefits of any time Roy spent with Yvonne and Gabriel was that he'd have several cousins nearby to play with.

Kris reminded himself he should be happy that Roy felt confident enough to be away from his dad for a day or two. That was impressive for the kid's young age.

Still, at times when Monica didn't need him by her side for a short time, he'd pop by to visit his son. He loved every moment spent with that boy. Even the admittedly exhausting and annoying ones.

Kris and Yvonne exchanged goodbyes, and he closed the app.

"I'm sorry to put you through this," Monica said quietly just as Ellis returned to his office carrying a tablet, a stack of file folders, and a coffee cup. "I'll move to a hotel tonight."

"Please don't." Kris had meant it when he'd said he wanted to make helping her his main priority until they solved this case and found her attackers. "If this goes on for very long, we can talk about different arrangements." It wouldn't be fair to ask his son to stay away from home for too long.

"What's this?" Ellis asked, stepping behind his desk and taking a sip of coffee from the oversized mug.

Kris summarized their conversation.

"If I end up having to bring the feds in to work alongside us on this and not just as a source of information, we might be able to get access to some type of safe house somewhere in the state," the chief said. "They must have something somewhere. And speaking of feds, I was just on the phone with both state and federal law enforcement agencies. Use of explosives is always especially concerning, so I gave them the details of what we learned last night about the device connected to the trailer door. The fed confirmed that the fairly simple pressure-triggered assembly made of easily obtainable items is relatively common as far as explosives go, and it doesn't point to any specific criminal or criminal group that he could think of off the top of his head. But they'll add the incident to their own databases along with the possible involvement of the Boyd Sierra syndicate, and he'll let me know if any connection or helpful information pops up."

Ellis tossed the items he'd been carrying onto his desk and sat down. "Detective Campbell has taken up the larger-scale investigation, and right now officers are keeping an eye out for the vehicle described in the initial attack," the chief said to Monica. "Now, I understand from Kris that you have something to tell me?"

Monica recapped what she'd told Kris last night about her plans to find what she needed to help her parents, including her visit to the Elk Ridge Resort as her first stop.

Kris's body tensed as he waited for the chief's

response. Ultimately, whether Kris could devote his on-duty time to protecting Monica and helping her with her search was up to Ellis. Whether he'd be allowed to continue offering Monica a place to stay at the ranch was up to his boss, too. Kris was aware that he was skirting a professional and personal line.

Ellis gazed at Monica for what felt like a long time before finally saying, "I can't prevent you from going through with your plans, but I can ask you to stop. For the sake of your own safety. So, will you stop?"

Monica sat up straighter, her posture and her jawline rigid. "No, sir. I will not."

Kris wanted her to be safe, but he also couldn't help admiring her determination and courage.

"I figured as much." Ellis leaned back in his chair. "I'll assign Officer Volker to be your security detail and to assist you for the time being. What's your next step?"

"I know which bank my dad used in town. I want to talk to the manager there. See if they'll confirm if he had a safe-deposit box where he might have left some kind of information on his former bosses."

Ellis frowned. "They won't tell you much without legal authorization from your father."

"I know," Monica said. "But if I can confirm that there's a safe-deposit box, then I'll get started learning how to get access to it."

Ellis nodded. "Okay, that's a good idea. What else have you got planned?"

"Esmeralda Marino is thinking about possible locations where my dad might have hidden something. Places she knows he was connected to when he was growing up here. She suggested I look around his childhood home, so I plan to do that. She said he might have had hiding places on the property as a kid that nobody would know about but him. She's also reaching out to people who knew my dad. Especially old friends. Maybe they have ideas. Maybe he confided in one of them."

And maybe all of this is a waste of time. Kris reminded himself that plenty of investigations started with no leads and few clues, but then things grew from there. Maybe some random bit of evidence along the way would bring them to information that was more substantial.

"Esmeralda has helped a lot of people in town, and she's worked with the police department in several situations without asking for anything in return," Ellis said. "There's no telling how many people are waiting for the opportunity to do something good for her, including getting her information that she's seeking. The news about the trailer explosion is all over town. That might make people even more willing to step up. I think you should make talking to her this morning your first priority."

"Okay," Monica said. "And after we talk to her, we can go by the bank."

Kris nodded in agreement.

They left the office and got into Kris's patrol car. Monica had just pulled out her phone when it rang, and she glanced at the screen. "It's Ryan, my dad's friend from the resort."

"Put it on speaker."

She frowned at him.

"If you and I are going to be working together on this, we need to trust each other, and we need to share information. It's better if I hear it directly rather than secondhand as much as possible. If Ryan's making a social call and it's not about the case, then obviously I don't need to hear it."

Her expression softened. "All right." She tapped the screen and shifted the call to the speaker setting. "Ryan, hello."

"Hey, are you okay? I saw the story about the trailer explosion. Of course, rumors are flying around town, but I heard your name connected to the reports. Is it true? Were you there? Was it targeted at you? I can hardly believe it." The words all came out in an anxious rush.

"Yes, I was there, and I'm fine," Monica told

him. "Not exactly the kind of thing you'd expect in Cedar Lodge, but I'm going to guess that you already know about my dad's criminal prosecution and the nature of the people he worked for."

"Sadly, I do know," Ryan said, his voice more subdued now.

"Ask him if he has any idea where your dad might have left something for safekeeping," Kris whispered.

She put the question to Ryan, and there was a pause at the other end of the call.

"Only thing that comes to mind is his old locker in the resort gym. But that would have been cleared out when his time-share interest was sold."

"Well, if you think of anything, please let me know."

"Of course."

The call ended, and then Monica tapped the screen to connect to Esmeralda.

Kris listened as the call went to voice mail. "Try again. Maybe she just couldn't get to the phone in time." She still didn't pick up.

"I'll try the thrift shop number," Monica said, tension creeping into her voice.

She'd talked to Esmeralda last night after the explosion. Of course her dear friend had been shocked. Monica had been adamant that she would not return to work despite Esmeralda's protests. She'd exposed her friend to more than enough danger.

Kris had already driven the patrol car to the edge of the driveway. He paused and checked out the side street beside the police facility before pulling out onto the street.

The call to the thrift shop continued to ring until it rolled over to a generic voice mail.

"She didn't mention closing the shop today," Monica said as she disconnected.

"Why don't you try her personal number again?"

Start Again Thrift was closer than her house to their current location. Concerned about Esmeralda's welfare, Kris decided to head there first. Tension tightened his stomach and he prayed that the woman so beloved in the community was okay.

The CLOSED sign hung in the window of Start Again Thrift. The interior lights were off save for one lone fixture always left on near the front door. There were no vehicles parked nearby other than Monica's sedan.

As she gazed at the burnt-out trailer that was to have been her temporary home, fear of what might have happened sent an eerie sensation of goose bumps rippling across her skin. It was followed by the horrifying thought that Esmeralda might have been targeted for attack because she'd helped Monica. Maybe that was why the store was unexpectedly closed and her friend was not answering her phone.

With her phone on speaker, Monica tried to call Esmeralda, but again the call rolled to voice mail. Monica exchanged a worried look with Kris.

He nodded. "We'll head to her house right now."

Moments later, Kris pulled to the curb in front of a sky blue clapboard house with a white picket fence, a front lawn edged in verdant shrubs and bright flowers, and Esmeralda's minivan parked in the driveway. The curtains for the picture window facing the street were tied back. At least one lamp glowed inside. After both Kris and Monica took a lingering look around to make sure it was safe, they got out of the car. Nothing seemed amiss as they walked up the pathway to the front door, with Kris continuing to vigilantly monitor their surroundings.

Nevertheless, Monica's heart beat heavier than usual in her chest under the weight of nervous concern. She didn't want to let the violent events of the last two days turn her into someone who lived her days tormented by fear, but concern for her friend was unavoidable. She offered up a silent prayer for Esmeralda's well-being.

Kris knocked on the white front door, barely waiting for a response before he turned to Monica and said, "Stay behind me." Then he opened the door, which was unlocked as usual, and cautiously stepped inside. "Hello?" he called out. "Esmeralda? Are you home? It's Kris."

There was no human response, but almost immediately, Monica heard the tapping sound of canine toenails hitting the hardwood floor.

A small white fluff ball of a dog with a few bits of grass clippings and dirt in its fur rounded a corner and then stopped short to offer a friendly yap.

Kris leaned down to give the dog a quick pet before continuing in the direction the tiny watchdog had come from. Monica couldn't see much from behind him. But then she saw the cop's broad shoulders visibly relax as he rounded the corner ahead of her. At that point, she could see the open glass slider door and Esmeralda at the edge of the lawn, on her knees, working in a flower bed.

A wave of relief hit Monica so hard she stumbled slightly.

"Hey!" Kris called as he stepped outside, with Monica following. "We've been trying to reach you on the phone."

Esmeralda startled and then turned, tipping her head back to see them from beneath the

brim of her floppy sun hat. She offered a con-
trite smile. "I hope I didn't worry you. I checked
in with my kids this morning so they wouldn't
be concerned, and then I came out here for a
little quiet time with the Lord and my flowers.
I intentionally left my phone in the kitchen so I
could have a couple of hours of peace."

She reached for her cane to help her stand. A
Siamese cat who had been sitting nearby scam-
pered a few feet away and then stopped to turn
and watch everything with luminous blue eyes.
Kris held out the crook of his arm, and Esmeralda took hold, allowing him to help her to her
feet.

"I didn't mean to snap at you," Kris said. "I
was just worried when you didn't answer your
phone and then we went by the shop and everything was locked up."

"It's all right." She smiled brightly and patted
his arm just before she let go of him. "I decided
to close the shop and let my employees have a
paid day off to come to grips with the explosion
and fire last night." By now her smile had faded.
"Of course, it happened shortly after we'd closed
up the store and left, but they're still upset. Understandably."

"Makes sense," Kris said.

"And it's not me these criminals are coming after." She turned to Monica. "It's you. And

you're the person we should be concerned about. How are you? Seriously. You've been through quite a lot."

"Better now that I know you're okay," Monica said.

The fluffy little dog reappeared and offered a couple more friendly barks.

"You're new around here," Kris said, reaching down to scoop up the critter and hold him against his chest.

"That's Rocky," Esmeralda said, smiling fondly at her pooch. "I've had him about two months, and he wants to be everybody's best friend." She began walking toward the house. "Let's go inside."

They settled in the living room after Kris and Monica politely declined Esmeralda's offer of something to drink.

"I know the full story of why Monica is remaining in town, so one of the reasons we were trying to track you down this morning was to find out if you've gotten any new ideas or tips on where we should look for information Hunter Larson might have documented and hidden regarding his criminal cronies."

Esmeralda leaned back in her floral print chair and clasped her hands in her lap. "I have put the word out, making sure to include my most busybody friends, but I haven't heard anything yet."

"We're going to check out Dad's old house today."

"I've been thinking some more about that, and he might not have left it in the actual house. There's lots of wooded area around that property where he could have put something. Buried it, maybe."

"How would I ever find it?"

"A metal detector?" Esmeralda shrugged. "Based on all the kids' adventure movies I watched as my children were growing up, I'd say search for something that would make a memorable landmark and stand the test of time. A distinctly shaped rock, or pile of rocks, something like that."

"Was your dad released on bail after he was initially arrested?" Kris asked.

Monica nodded.

"So he could have come up to Cedar Lodge and buried something shortly before his trial when he realized he was going to be convicted and locked up. And that would have been, what, about a year ago? We could look for ground that appears as if it's been disturbed relatively recently."

"All of this assuming the owners allow us access to the property," Monica said.

Kris settled his gaze on her. "I think it's worth a try."

He was right.

"Let's go have a look after we stop at the bank to find out if Dad had a safe-deposit box."

With no better ideas, and so much at stake, they had to pursue every potential lead they could think of. And they needed to do it quickly. The longer this was drawn out, the more she and her family and friends—like Esmeralda—would be exposed to danger.

SIX

"I'm afraid it's against policy for me to give you any information about our clients. Or to even confirm if your father is one of our clients," the bank employee said.

Monica gave a slight nod of understanding as she tried to rein in her frustration. Not with the woman sitting at a desk in front of her in an office cubicle in the bank. But frustration with the situation overall.

She'd tried not to get her hopes up as they'd driven to the bank from Esmeralda's house. It was common knowledge that banks didn't give out depositors' information freely. Still, she had allowed herself a little bit of hope.

"May I offer a suggestion?" the bank employee asked.

"Sure."

"Get a certified power of attorney from your father. With that in hand, most banks will answer your questions and work with you. Us included."

In the blur of activity after her father's arrest and subsequent posting of bail, Monica had accompanied her father on one of his visits with his attorney. She'd signed some things, been shown some documents, and was fairly certain she did have power of attorney. But she hadn't thought about it since then. She didn't think she had an actual copy of it, paper or digitized. And obtaining that would take time.

"What if I have his authorization but I don't have the safe-deposit box key?" Monica asked.

"The lock can be drilled and the box opened. There's a fee for that."

There might be a fee to contact the lawyer for the certified documentation she needed, too. And how certain was she that her dad's attorney was not connected to the Boyd Sierra Associates criminal group?

Not certain at all.

As they stepped out of the bank into bright sunlight, Kris moved in front of Monica to keep her behind him for a few moments until he'd taken a cautious look around. Then they continued to the patrol car and got in.

"Do you think this might be a good time to contact your mother and see if she has any information or documentation that might help?"

Monica shook her head. "The last thing she wants to do is help me find evidence that her fiancé is a crook. And I can't help thinking she would tell Archer what was going on. If he suspected she might be helping me—even if she wasn't—that could put her in danger."

"Might as well call your dad's attorney's office and see what they can do for you," Kris said while they sat in the parked police car.

Monica had the attorney listed in her directory. She placed a call and spoke with a paralegal, who listened to Monica's request for information and told her she'd get back to her later, despite Monica emphasizing that this was an urgent and time-sensitive request.

"Okay," Monica said after the disappointingly short and unfruitful conversation. "Let's move on to our next step and drive out to my dad's old house."

Kris reached for his phone. "Let me check in with the chief first."

"Put it on speaker so I can hear," Monica said, feeling a slight smile lift the corner of her mouth. "We *are* a team now, right?"

"Yes, we are." He smiled faintly without looking at her.

He's a good cop and kind person just doing his job, she told herself after her heart seemed to skip a beat at the sight of his smile. This partnership wasn't going anywhere. Not beyond getting a job done.

Ellis picked up the call. "What have you got to report, Kris?"

"Not much. We can't get information about Hunter Larson at the bank without jumping through some legal hoops. The process has been started but will take time."

"What I expected."

"Esmeralda didn't have any new information or suggestions, but she's still asking around. Right now we're going to head to Hunter Larson's childhood home."

"Good. Campbell and his team are working their confidential informants and also visiting hardware stores to see if anyone remembers selling the items that were used for the explosive device on the trailer. We haven't gotten a hit on the search for the SUV involved in the attack at the Bennett cabin fire, but we're still looking."

After the call ended, Kris pulled away from the curb and drove through downtown. He took a couple of turns that ended with them heading southwest toward a more sparsely populated area. The road quickly became hilly and tree-lined, with jagged snowcapped peaks visible in the distance. Occasionally they crossed a stretch of the winding Meadowlark River.

"My dad always said he loved it here, but

there just weren't the financial opportunities he wanted as a young man," Monica said, pondering the amazing beauty of the area. "Financial opportunities were of supreme importance to him until everything started unraveling and he realized he'd gone too far."

"I understand wanting to go see the world," Kris said. "But when I left for the army, I knew I'd come back. And my late wife and I both wanted to raise Roy here."

"Do you hope to expand your family?" *Subtle, Monica.* She cringed a little, but the question had just popped out.

He gave a half shrug. "Between working as a cop and helping at the ranch, my time with Roy is limited enough as it is. I'm not willing to take any more time away from him to date."

Embarrassment heated her cheeks. It sounded as if he was making it clear that he wasn't interested in her. Well, she wasn't interested in him.

Not anymore.

So why had disappointment dropped hard into her stomach like a stale doughnut?

From the corner of her eye, she watched Kris's head move as he shifted his gaze to the rearview mirror and side mirror and then back to the road in front of them.

The feverish, jittery unease that had plagued Monica after the cabin attack yesterday flared up, demanding her attention. She wanted to believe that being in the company of a lawman guaranteed her safety, but Kris's constant vigilance reminded her that simply wasn't true.

"Do you really think someone would have the nerve to tail a patrol car?" she asked while taking a glance at her own side mirror.

"Not usually. But in this case, I'm afraid they might try."

They crested a rise in the road, and Monica was stunned to see an entire development of pricey-looking houses spread across the stretch of flatland and up over the nearby hillside.

"This…is so different from how it looked the last time I was here." She fumbled for words because this used to be a small community of modest homes owned by working-class families dependent on income from the nearby granite quarry. Now, as they drove down the road, she spotted expensive vehicles, trendy stores, and the outpost of a chain coffee shop she would never have expected to see on the fringes of Cedar Lodge, Montana.

"Things change," Kris said. "We have to roll with that fact, like it or not."

She glanced over, intrigued by his tone. It sounded as if he might be thinking about his own personal life and the loss of his wife more than the challenges faced by dramatic changes in a community.

Either way, they needed to stay focused on the task at hand so that she could find the information she needed and head back to Reno, and Kris's young son could move back home to the ranch.

Kris took a turn from the highway, heading deeper into the community toward the intersection of streets that Esmeralda had suggested to Monica as a good starting place. He pulled into the parking lot of an elementary school. "Which way from here?"

"I'm not sure." Monica took a couple of photos of their surroundings and sent them to Esmeralda.

Moments later, Esmeralda called. "Now that I'm looking at the pictures I can remember exactly how to get to your dad's old house from there." She rattled off the directions and ended by encouraging them to be careful and to call her if they needed more help.

Kris pulled out of the parking lot and resumed driving.

After making a series of turns the road changed, becoming wider and smoother. It appeared that the improvements had been made recently.

When they reached the street at the base of the hill where Esmeralda told them they'd find the old house, they were facing a development of new condominiums instead.

"This was it," Monica said dully. "Now that we're here I remember the neighborhood more clearly. This was the spot where my dad lived as a kid."

Kris turned into one of the development parking lots.

Banners tied to poles stuck in the ground and hanging from a couple of second-story balconies advertised the properties for sale.

"The house used to be there." Monica pointed to a spot between a set of dark wood condos. A small body of water was visible a little farther away. "There's the pond that used to be in back of the house."

Driving closer, Kris could see that the pond was now part of a landscaped common area with a wooden walkway around it and a couple of picnic tables on the surrounding grassy area.

"This all looks so new. It must have been done in the last few months," Monica said. "Even if Dad buried something in the ground before he went to prison, it would have been dug up or destroyed when all of this was constructed."

"I think you're right."

She reached up to rub the right side of her

head. "This is so frustrating. I wish I could remember what my dad told me." Then she turned to Kris. "What if I've gotten everything wrong? Maybe the notes on my phone showing that I'd researched making a road trip to Cedar Lodge had nothing to do with any of this?" She blew out a puff of air. "I'm sorry for wasting your time."

"It happens. Running up against a dead end sometimes is part of investigative work. And this dead end right here doesn't mean you were wrong to come to Cedar Lodge."

"I suppose." She looked around. "Should we get out and walk around the property on the off chance we actually can find something?" she asked. "Since we're here."

Kris shook his head. "When we talked about doing this, I imagined you looking around inside a house or in a forested area surrounding the house where you'd be hidden from view." He glanced in his mirrors as he'd done the whole trip, and gazed at the nearby parking lot and buildings, as well. "This is too open and exposed. Without a specific reason to think there's been something important buried around here, it's not worth the risk." The Boyd Sierra syndicate had the financial resources to hire excellent help. Despite Kris's vigilance, it was possible they'd been followed from downtown by an expert who'd managed to stay out of view.

"Unless you've got some other thoughts on where to look, I'll take you back to the ranch, and then I'll head back to the police station for the rest of my shift."

She sighed heavily. "Right now I'm all out of ideas."

After they'd driven a couple of miles down the road, Monica said, "If I haven't made any headway with this in the next day or two, I'll move out of your ranch house. I realize you didn't plan on my staying forever."

"Let's just take this one day at a time," Kris responded.

"I know you must miss seeing your son."

"I do. But he loves staying with his other grandparents." And the truth was, Kris had repeatedly promised Yvonne and Gabriel that he would send Roy to their house more often for visits, but he hadn't followed through on that. He was aware that Roy was not simply their beloved grandson but also a living link to the daughter they still mourned. He'd been selfish. And now was a good time to stop that.

But he still planned to stop by and see Roy today if at all possible.

"Can we go by the thrift store?" Monica asked when they were out of the hinterlands and back downtown on Glacier Street. "I'd like to move my car to the ranch. Or at least get my suitcases out of the trunk."

"I'd rather not take the chance of someone seeing you drive your car to the ranch. Then they'll know where you're staying. Maybe just grab your stuff."

He turned into the thrift store parking lot so he could drive completely around the building to see if anyone was lurking nearby. Of course, Monica's car was the only vehicle there since the store was closed. He stopped several feet away.

"Can you open the trunk remotely?" he asked while they were both still in the patrol car.

She pulled a fob out of the cross-body bag she was wearing. "It will pop free of the latch, but it won't open all the way."

"Good enough."

She gave him a questioning look, so he glanced at the burned husk of the trailer and then turned back to her. "If somebody can rig an explosive to the trailer door, they can rig one to your car, too."

Eyes widened, she nodded. She hit the trunk unlock button, and Kris breathed a sigh of relief when nothing exploded. They got out and walked to her car, but before Kris could grab the suitcases from the trunk, Monica walked toward a rear passenger door. "I'm going to grab my laptop from the back, too."

"Wait!"

She froze and turned to face him.

"Stand back and unlock the doors. Then let me have a quick look around before you open any of them."

She pressed the fob, it beeped, and nothing happened. Still, Kris couldn't release the tightness in his chest. While serving in war zones, he'd seen too many instances where an area seemed safe, only for a bomb to be triggered when a person touched something that appeared completely innocuous.

He took a quick look at the thin coating of dust on the side of the car and the hood, searching for handprints or smudges or any sign that someone had tampered with the vehicle. Nothing. He searched the ground around the car. There were cracks in the asphalt with blades of grass poking up through, and none of them appeared bent or recently trod upon. "Looks good." He pulled open the unlocked door himself. No explosion.

Even then, he couldn't relax. He scanned the surrounding area, something he'd already done at least five times since they'd arrived. "Let's make this quick."

He walked back to the trunk and grabbed her suitcases just before he heard the roar of an engine and the squeal of tires. He stepped aside to look past the raised trunk lid and saw a dark sedan careening into the parking lot and racing full bore toward Monica's car.

Heart pounding in his chest, he yelled to Monica. Before he could take more than a couple of steps toward her, the speeding vehicle collided with the front of her car. The sound of the impact was a sickening crash of crunching metal and screeching tires. He was forced to leap out of the way as Monica's car spun under the force of the collision.

"Monica!" Kris scrambled to his feet and sprinted toward the side of the car where he'd last seen her, though now it was facing a different direction.

Gears shrieked and the engine growled as the attacking car backed up, preparing to bash Monica's car again.

Kris found Monica hanging halfway out the car door, tangled up in the dangling shoulder harness of a seat belt and a deployed airbag.

"Monica!"

For a moment, she didn't move. Fear twisted into a tight ball in Kris's stomach. Was she unconscious? Was she alive? Had her neck been broken?

"What happened?" she murmured weakly as Kris shoved the shoulder harness and deflating airbag aside and slid his arm under her shoulders. In a perfect situation, he wouldn't move her until he knew the extent of the injuries, but there was no time for being cautious right now.

"You got hit by a car, and he's coming back. We've got to move, *now*!"

Kris heard the grinding of the other car's engine as it roared toward them. Glancing up, he could see it barreling at them through the puzzle-piece pattern of the cracked safety glass in the windshield.

With Monica in his arms, he took several steps backward as quickly as he could before the next impact, this one bashing the front of the car into the back, collapsing the space where Monica would have been if he hadn't gotten her free.

Thank You, Lord.

A slight ease of relief moved through him when he realized Monica had gotten her footing and she could at least partially hold her own weight. They had to get moving. They were exposed here, backed up to the thrift shop's exterior brick wall, and they needed to get to cover before the attacking car came after them again.

"Can you make it to the patrol car?" Kris asked, his hands still gripping her in case she didn't have as much strength as he'd thought.

She nodded. "I think so."

The attacker car remained where it had ended up after the last assault, its own front end and right fender damaged. The vehicle made grinding and metallic squealing noises but didn't go anywhere. It sounded like the driver wanted to move but couldn't.

Kris tried to get a look at whoever was behind the wheel, but the tint of the windshield and the sunlight reflecting off it made that difficult. Fearful that the driver would get frustrated and pull out a gun and start shooting, Kris redirected his efforts back to getting Monica and himself back into his police cruiser.

"Let's go!" Kris had a shotgun accessible once they got into his vehicle. He would use it if the attacker tried to crash into the heavier, reinforced patrol car.

They began moving, Monica's balance unsteady and her feet stumbling, when again Kris heard the roar of an engine. Confused, since the original attacker was still stalled in place, he realized the sound was coming from the direction of the entrance on the opposite side of the parking lot.

In an instant, a full-size blue van gunned toward them, clearly intending to mow them down before they could reach the cop car.

Had the two attackers from the cabin fire each found new vehicles?

Desperate to keep Monica alive, Kris hadn't yet been able to free up his hands long enough to call for assistance. With the van barreling toward them, he couldn't do that now. And with everything happening so fast they didn't have enough time to cover the short distance to his patrol unit.

"The trailer!"

It looked brittle and flimsy after the fire. Clambering inside it probably wouldn't offer much help. But if they could get to the back side of it, where there was a narrow space between the trailer and a cinder-block wall, maybe it would provide refuge long enough for Kris to radio for help and his fellow cops to respond.

They moved as quickly as they could. The lumbering van, which wasn't exactly designed for agile maneuvers, couldn't turn in time and it rocketed past them.

They were just rounding the edge of the trailer to get behind it when Kris heard the crack of a gunshot. Exactly what he'd feared.

Behind the less-than-ideal barrier, Kris freed his right hand from clasping Monica's arm. He grabbed his radio and called in the attack.

Within seconds, he heard sirens in the distance.

Nearby, more gunshots cracked. Kris hunkered down with Monica, holding her head close to his chest and covering it with his arms.

Finally the shooting stopped. Kris heard the growl of the van's engine fading as it sped away before he could get a clear look at the license plate.

The increasing wails of the sirens indicated that help was almost there.

Daring to release a small sigh of relief, Kris looked down at Monica still clutched in his arms and saw blood on the side of her face.

SEVEN

A robust fire crackled in the fireplace of the family room at the Volker ranch, but Monica still felt chilled to the bone. Several hours had passed since the attack behind the thrift store, but residual anxiety plagued her, making it hard for her to feel anything beyond cold fear.

She was seated on a sofa, feet up and leaning back to rest her stiff neck and shoulder on an oversized pillow. After this attack, Kris's friend Cole had been relentless in badgering Monica to get checked out at the hospital emergency room until she'd finally given in. The doctor had confirmed she had no life-threatening injuries, but she did have sore, strained muscles, a pounding headache, and a few cuts and scratches. Afterward, she and Kris had given their official statements to the police, and Kris was given the remainder of his shift off so that they could both go back to the ranch and get some rest.

It was early evening. The sky had clouded

over, and the temperature had dropped. Dinner had been homemade beef barley soup and grilled cheese sandwiches. Monica glanced over at Kris, who was seated in an easy chair, video-chatting with Roy. Jill and Pete were in their home office at the other end of the sprawling ranch house, going over some business issues related to their horse ranch. The Volker family had been so incredibly kind to her. They'd been a blessing she couldn't have even imagined before she hit town.

Sighing heavily, she reminded herself that despite the terrible events, she had a lot to appreciate, even if at the moment she didn't exactly *feel* grateful. What she felt was sore and scared, frustrated and confused, and nearly as angry with her dad as she'd been when he was first arrested and charged with fraud, theft, and participation in a criminal conspiracy.

Realizing she'd probably been looking at Kris a little too long, she shifted her gaze back to the window and the heavy gray clouds outside. Then back to the flickering flames in the fireplace.

Thank You, Lord, for Your protection. Thank You for the generous and helpful people You have brought into my life. Thank You for the gift of faith to help see me through all of this.

As had happened to her on so many prior occasions, her prayers of gratitude offered in faith

stirred to life the genuine feeling of thankful-
ness in her heart.

Her phone rang, startling her. Kris looked
in her direction, and she grabbed the device to
glance at the screen. "It's Esmeralda," she said
quietly.

"Dad. *Dad.*" Roy's voice came through the
tablet Kris was holding.

"You keep talking to your son," Monica told
Kris softly. "I'll let you know what Esmeralda
has to say."

After a slight hesitation, Kris nodded and
turned back to the screen and his son.

The warm domesticity of the moment hit
Monica without warning. A cozy house. A man
talking to his little boy—even if it was via tech-
nology—by her side. A delicate wisp of a feeling
she'd craved in various forms for a long time.
First as a child, when she'd wished for siblings
and nearby cousins to play with and parents who
were more interested in family activities. And
later, when she'd decided to earn a teaching cre-
dential so that she could work with children and
help them learn and thrive in life.

There wasn't much chance of any of that
working out for real now that she had a criminal
father and mob assailants trying to kill her. Oh,
and one slightly more sophisticated thug doing
his best to manipulate her mother into marriage.

She shook her head, trying to discard the feelings, and got a reminder of her sore neck in the process.

"Hey, Esmeralda," she said after tapping the screen of her phone. "How are you?"

"How am *I*? Honey, I waited as long as I could to give you time to rest and then find out how *you* are."

"Sore and shaken up. But it could have been much worse."

Monica gave a brief recap of the attack and mentioned that Kris had asked a friend to tow her car and store it on his property in town. The attacker's wrecked car—which had been stolen—had been impounded by the police while they swept it for evidence.

"The trip to Dad's old house was a bust," Monica said at the end of the update. "The house and trees have been knocked down for condos. The pond is still there. I suppose it's possible Dad hid something in there, but I don't think it's likely."

"I should have anticipated that," Esmeralda said. "I haven't been out that way in ages, but Cedar Lodge has doubled in population in the last few years. Things are bound to be different."

"True enough."

"I'm also calling to offer another suggestion. It's not a location to search for hidden documents, but a person for you to talk to. Your dad's best friend growing up. You ever heard him mention a guy named Brendan Stryker?"

Monica thought for a moment. "Brendan does seem familiar." But a specific instance of her dad mentioning him didn't come to mind. Maybe she was trying to convince herself it sounded familiar because she so desperately wanted to get somewhere with all of this and find the proof of Archer Nolan's criminal nature and activities.

"One of my nephews who's about the same age as your dad said he remembered Hunter and Brendan being buddies from middle school through high school. My nephew's going to try and get contact information for Brendan, and I'll pass that along to you."

"I appreciate it."

They spoke a few more minutes and then disconnected, and Monica related the information to Kris, who had just ended his video call with Roy.

"When I get to the police department tomorrow, I'll see what kind of information I can pull up on Brendan."

"It's worth trying to talk to him." They didn't have any other viable options at this point, so they needed to follow through on even the weakest of leads.

Monica's phone chimed the arrival of a text. "It's Ryan," she said. She tapped to open it and read it aloud: "'Just wrapped up work and saw what happened on the local news app. Man, these people are relentless. The guy who does a lot of the paving work at the resort, Jason Mulhern, has a criminal record and he knew your dad. Maybe check him out? Also, remembered some kind of business group your dad met with when he was here. Will think about it and try to remember details.'"

Kris nodded. "I'll check out Mulhern, and if he comes up with something on the business group, I'll follow up on that, too."

The implication seemed to be that he would do it alone. Without Monica.

"*We* will follow up on it," she said. Right now it was tempting to hide out someplace safe while the whole horrible situation got resolved. But doing that would not help. It would only slow things down. "You don't know my dad," Monica said. "I have a frame of reference with knowledge that you lack. Timelines in my dad's life. Familiar places. Familiar names. Someone could mention a small detail that would seem insignificant to you, but it would be meaningful to me. I could add it to other information and see a pattern where you couldn't."

"It's your call," he finally said.

It was. It was her decision if she was willing to put herself in danger, despite her fears.

"This doesn't have to be your fight," she said, thinking about Kris's exposure to the attackers today. He hadn't been injured, but he could have been.

"Of course it's my fight." He squared his shoulders. "This isn't just about you and your dad. A criminal syndicate has people launching attacks in my town. There are too many people that I care about in Cedar Lodge to turn away and let the thugs do what they want."

His heated words encouraged a sprout of hope in her heart. The hope that she would get the information she needed to solve her problems.

There was another small hope also alive in her heart that she didn't dare encourage.

She had no chance of a future with Kris and his family, even if she did feel a growing sense of warmth and connection with all of them. Even if she felt like she and Kris understood one another in a way that was more than friendship. Looking at him now, she couldn't stop her heart from beating faster and her stomach from fluttering with a silly burst of delight.

But he might not feel the same way about her.

Beyond that, a cop didn't need the daughter of a convicted criminal in his life. And after everything that had happened, no school in town would ever hire her.

She would continue her effort at uncovering

information while doing her best to keep Kris and herself physically safe.

She would keep her heart safe, too.

"Try to get some rest today," Kris said to Monica the next morning as she wandered into the kitchen shortly after sunrise.

He turned to the coffeepot on the counter to refill his thermos mug and add a splash of cream before snapping the lid into place. "I've got to put in a few hours working patrol, and while I'm at the station, I'll check on Brendan Stryker and see what I can find out." He poured a second cup of coffee and offered it to her. She stared back at him with a dull expression before taking a few slurps of coffee, and then she appeared to wake up a little more.

Kris had learned after Monica's first night at the ranch that she wasn't a morning person, but coffee seemed to help brighten her up. This morning it looked like it might take a lot to do the trick.

"If I sit around and rest, I'll be miserable," she finally said. She slumped into a chair at the kitchen table. A few strands of her unruly blond locks had sprung free from her tied-back hair, and there were dark circles under her eyes. "If I'm not busy, my mind races with all the terrible what-ifs I can think of." She took another sip of coffee.

"I'm familiar with that situation." Time spent in combat while in the army was not something Kris had been able to walk away from and quickly forget. "Prayer can help a lot."

"You're right." She nodded sagely and then gave a self-deprecating laugh, shaking her head. "I hand things over to God, but then, before I know it, I've picked them right back up again."

"As soon as you realize you've done that, pray again. That's my best advice. Not that you asked for it."

Jill pulled open the door that led into the kitchen from the mudroom, toed off a pair of work boots, and then walked over to the sink to wash her hands. "The animals are fed and watered, and I think we've earned some breakfast."

Kris smiled at his mom. Of course she'd already been awake and at work for hours. "Give me a few minutes and I'll put together a skillet scramble with some eggs and bacon," Jill said.

"I'm about to leave for the station shortly," Kris replied from his spot leaning against the counter. "Can you clear your schedule to hang out in the house with Monica until early afternoon?"

"I'm sure I'll be fine," Monica interjected. She glanced over at Betty lying on a dog bed. As usual, the old hound interpreted eye contact as a beckon to be petted, and she got up and lumbered over to Monica. Not to be left out, Pepper pushed himself up off the hardwood floor where he'd been splayed and pranced over to Monica so she could pet him, too.

"I don't mind staying in the house," Jill called out as she started grabbing things from the refrigerator. "I've got some bookkeeping to catch up on, and I want to get a batch of whole wheat bread started."

"How do you run this ranch with just the three of you?" Monica asked.

"We're not at full capacity right now." Kris was determined to fight the temptation to linger and chat with Monica.

"We're boarding a few horses and doing some training while saving up and getting ready to expand the operation," Jill added.

Kris was happy that Monica and his mom seemed to be developing a friendship. But at the same time, he hadn't forgotten why Monica was here and that they all needed to remain vigilant.

If he really wanted to help Monica, he needed to get out and do what he could to put an end to the attacks. If he was able to spend a little time at the police station before going out, he might be able to research Brendan Stryker and the paving company guy as well as sit in on Detective

Campbell's update to the chief on how his investigation was going.

"All right, I'm leaving." Kris pushed himself away from the counter and grabbed his coffee mug. "Call me if either of you needs anything."

He gave Betty a scratch behind the ears as he walked by her. Pepper was over by Jill, keeping an eagle eye out for any tasty food morsel that Kris's mom might accidentally drop while making breakfast.

He stepped outside and paused on the front porch for a moment to look around. Of course, he'd viewed the security video feed a short time ago, but he wasn't taking any chances. Seeing nothing out of the ordinary near the house, he turned his attention toward the nearest corral. He watched his dad open a gate to the pasture, letting the horses out to run and kick and enjoy the cool grass and space to trot around.

Early-morning sunlight blazed along the tips of the jagged hilltops and ridges that were part of the Volker family property. Kris was blessed to live here. He was blessed to have survived his tours of combat, to have his family, to have his son, and to have had Angela in his life. He felt that painful spark that so often sliced into his heart when he thought of his late wife. And on the heels of that, he felt something else, heavy and unsettling. It took him a moment to realize what it was. Guilt.

He felt guilty because he was seriously attracted to Monica. He didn't just think she was pretty. It was something much more than that.

How could this be possible? Angela had been the love of his life. He'd known it, and he'd told her so more times than he could count. If he could move on to another woman now, did that mean what he'd declared to Angela had been a lie?

He stepped off the porch and walked toward his patrol car. Normally he used his truck to go back and forth to work and only used his police unit when on shift. But these were not normal times. Not for his town. Not for the woman he would help and then see on her way after the job was finished and they both returned to their normal lives.

He heard the front door open and close. He turned to see his mom walking toward him carrying a paper bag. "Here." She shoved the bag at him. "It's a couple of leftover biscuits split with a slice of ham and cheddar cheese in each one."

"Thanks, Mom."

She leaned in to give him a kiss on the cheek. And then she lingered, taking a step back, arms crossed.

If his mom had something to say, Kris knew

he would hear it sooner rather than later. "*What*, Mom?"

Cocking her head to one side, she smiled slightly and said, "She's a lovely young woman, isn't she?"

"Monica? Yeah, sure."

"It's nice to see you interested in someone. Even if you met under extreme circumstances."

"*Interested?*" He realized he'd raised his voice and adjusted his volume before adding, "She's not here because I'm interested. She's here because she's got no other options, and if she checked into a hotel, she probably wouldn't live to see another day."

"Son, give me credit for having a few brains in my head. I know what I see right in front of me."

"Now you sound smug."

She shrugged. "Looks to me like she's interested in you, too."

He shook his head. "You're getting your hopes up over nothing." Kris was determined not to do the same. That pointed edge of guilt he'd felt earlier stabbed at him again. "Besides, no one will ever take Angela's place."

"Who said anything about taking someone's place?" This time it was Jill who raised her voice. "More than one thing can be true at once. You realize that, right?" Her voice dropped in volume. "Son, you can love and honor Angela's memory *and* find someone to share your life with for however much time God gives you. Angela *told* you she hoped you would find someone else after she was gone. I heard her say it. More than once."

Kris nodded but didn't speak. His throat closed up with emotion. His mom wasn't wrong. But the present moment wasn't a good time to process all of this. "It still hurts to think about Angela being gone," he finally said, practically forcing out the words. "It doesn't seem fair to a woman to bring her into my life if I still feel that way."

Jill reached for his hands. "You take all the time you need to work through your grief. But since you seem to like Monica, let me give you just a little push."

Kris laughed. *Take your time, but let me give you a little push* pretty much summed up his mom.

"I have Roy, Mom. He's the most important thing in my life. With my job and helping out at the ranch, I don't spend nearly enough time with him. I don't have time to date. And I really don't want to." Awkward dinners with a woman he barely knew, away from his son? Going on *fun* outings where he spent the whole time wondering what his boy was doing? No thanks.

Jill made a scoffing sound. "That boy is your shadow when you're here working the ranch.

The right woman will want to get to know Roy. And be patient as she lets him get to know her."

"I don't know, Mom." Kris looked up at the vibrant blue sky before turning back to her. "There's an awful lot going on right now. And I need to get to work." He glanced over at the horses happily munching on grass. His dad was leaning against the outside of the stable, using a garden hose to rinse off the bottoms of his rubber work boots. Kris breathed in and could smell the cedar and aspen and pines growing on the nearby mountainside. He knew enough to enjoy a beautiful moment. Because it could all disappear in an instant.

Images from last night's attack played through his mind. Monica had nearly been killed. And there was no sign the assailants were going to let up on their attacks.

"If you see or hear anything out of the ordinary, let me know." He got into the patrol car and started down the driveway, determined to get his focus back on the job he needed to do. He had to help Monica find her answers while keeping her alive. The emotions tugging at him when he was around her were unimportant.

Doing his job and taking care of Roy. *That* was what mattered.

EIGHT

As he left the late-afternoon meeting at the police station, Kris found himself more worried than ever about Monica's safety.

He'd thought he understood the dangerous reach of the Boyd Sierra crime syndicate. But according to the report he'd just gotten from a federal agent via video call, the syndicate had a large network of sophisticated contract killers they could send to Cedar Lodge. It included young and older female assassins who were proficient at approaching their target without setting off anyone's intuitive safety alarms until it was too late. The clock was ticking to get this case wrapped up before the Boyd Sierra leadership decided to make Monica's death its highest priority.

Shortly before the meeting ended, he'd sent Monica a text letting her know that he'd checked up on Brendan Stryker and learned where he worked. He asked her to be ready to go talk to the man when Kris got back to the ranch. While Detective Campbell and his team continued their standard police investigation, Chief Ellis wanted Kris to continue protecting Monica and working with her to find the evidence she thought her father had hidden somewhere in town, even though no one, not even Monica, had a clue as to what it might tell them.

Traffic was sparse on the highway driving back to the ranch, and Kris was grateful. He hoped to take Monica to talk to Brendan and then return to the ranch before it got completely dark. He glanced out the window at the lowering sun. It would be pushing it. Nighttime driving made it hard to spot anyone tailing them. The only thing visible would be headlights. His former hope that the bad guys might hesitate to tail—or even attack—a patrol car was obviously now gone. Yesterday's nearly deadly demolition derby behind the thrift store made it clear *anything* could happen as the assailants pulled out all the stops to get to Monica.

He turned onto the driveway at the ranch, taking it a little too fast and bumping and jostling along the way. One of the outside dogs, Alfie, raced across the pasture with what looked like a rawhide bone in his mouth. Lily, smaller than Alfie but younger and more energetic, chased after him. A trio of horses stood together near a corral fence as if having a conversation. Despite the concern nipping at Kris and keeping him worried about Monica, now that he'd returned to the ranch, he was able to let go of some of the tension in his tight neck and shoulder muscles and let his body relax. Everything looked fine.

Looks can be deceiving.

That familiar whisper had spoken to him many times in the past when he was a soldier patrolling war-torn regions overseas where it was nearly impossible to anticipate what might happen next. And a few times in equally uncertain situations here in Cedar Lodge, too.

He took a good look around as he got out of his patrol car. Satisfied for the moment that things were quiet and normal, he walked up into the house. The first thing he noticed when he yanked open the front door was the beef and potato scent of shepherd's pie baking in the oven. The second thing he noticed was Monica perched at the edge of a chair in the living room, cross-body bag across her shoulder, clearly anxious to go talk to Brendan.

"What are they saying at the police department?" Monica asked as soon as he'd said hello to her and called out a greeting to his parents in the kitchen.

"Have they got any new information?" Pete asked, walking into the living room, picking up their calico cat, Penny, and then sitting down with her in his lap.

Jill also came around from the kitchen while wiping her hands with a dish towel. She leaned against the doorway to listen.

Kris sat in the chair across from Monica. Like her, he was anxious to get going. But his parents had opened up their home to a complete stranger and taken on the risks associated with that, so they deserved to hear the information he had. He would make it quick.

"Good news on a couple of fronts," Kris started. "The involvement of the Boyd Sierra criminal enterprise has attracted the attention of state and federal agencies, and they're offering help. Right now it's only in the form of whatever supportive investigative work they can do online. They aren't sending agents to Cedar Lodge, but it's something.

"Beyond that, we've learned the car that rammed Monica's sedan yesterday was stolen. No surprise there. Images of the van were picked up on a security camera farther up Glacier Street, and it was stolen, too. Both vehicles were taken from the same part of town, and we've got officers reviewing home security video from that neighborhood. There's a chance the thugs are staying somewhere in that area, so officers will be checking hotels and short-term rentals in the neighborhood, too. Maybe someone will have noticed something helpful."

"That's some good news," Pete said, scratching the cat in his lap behind the ears. "What's the bad news?"

Kris smiled faintly. His dad wasn't a pessimist, but he *was* a realist. Ranch life did that to a person.

Kris turned to Monica. "The feds who have been building a case strong enough to completely take down Boyd Sierra Associates believe the criminals will double down on their efforts to get to you. The fact that your dad decided to leave them and is now willing to turn on them and hand over information to the authorities is a huge blow. No one in that kind of position with the syndicate has ever done that before. If you and your dad are even partially successful in your endeavor, it will make the association look weak to their criminal underground enemies, and they can't have that."

Monica wore a troubled expression. "I guess I wanted to believe that this was happening because Archer Nolan wants to marry my mom and that he had hired a couple of goons to come after me. I didn't want it to be an issue involving the entire syndicate."

Kris got to his feet, and Monica mirrored his move.

"So, where are we going to find Brendan?" Monica asked.

"Fast Engine Car Repair. It's on the south side of town near the river."

They walked out onto the front porch. Kris stepped in front of Monica and took a good look around before escorting her to his patrol car.

Security cameras and alert farm dogs had originally made him assume the Double V Ranch would be a safe haven for her. But now, as he glanced toward the forest on the edge of the pasture and the mountain ridges that rose up behind the house, he couldn't help thinking about the resources at the disposal of the criminal syndicate intent on killing her.

One high-powered rifle in the hands of a skilled shooter could take her out.

The sun was barely lingering above the horizon as Kris pulled up to the curb in front of Fast Engine Car Repair. Monica glanced out her window at the repair bays visible through open roll-up doors, and it looked like most of the employees were gone for the day. The parking lot near the office door was empty.

After a cautious look around, they got out of the patrol car and walked up the sloping drive to one of the open repair bays. A thickset man in blue coveralls walked up to them just before they got inside. "Can I help you?"

Kris quickly stepped between Monica and the man. Monica moved slightly to the side so she could see around him.

For a moment, the man's gaze appeared to settle on the badge pinned to Kris's uniform. Then he slowly nodded, looking none too happy. His eyes flickered between Kris and Monica before focusing on the cop again. "I heard you might be coming out here, and I've got nothing to say to you."

"Good evening," Kris said in an easy tone. "I'm Officer Volker, and this is Monica Larson."

"I've got nothing to do with that mob criminal Hunter Larson." The man's tense stance and tight facial expression matched the borderline hostility of his words. "I'm an honest businessman, and I run an honest shop."

"You must be Brendan Stryker," Kris said calmly as if the outburst hadn't happened. "We're not here to accuse you of anything."

"You'd better not be. If you want to question me, you'll do it in front of my lawyer." He crossed his arms over his chest, still clenching an oily shop rag.

"I heard you and my dad used to be best friends," Monica offered, feeling a slight quiver in the pit of her stomach despite having Kris here to protect her. Brendan and his anger were intimidating.

Brendan stared at her for a minute. "You look like him," he finally said.

Monica tried to relax, hoping a soothing demeanor would get her some answers. "Look, I know my dad broke the law, and he's paying for his actions. Maybe you're disappointed in him because of that. But right now, I'm trying to track down information that could put more of the criminals he worked with behind bars. And yeah, full disclosure, providing that information to the authorities might get my dad a lighter sentence. But that's not the only reason I'm doing this. The entire situation is…*complicated*."

She hadn't meant to give a mini speech, but the words poured out, and she was determined to have her say before Brendan kicked them out of his shop.

His expression relaxed slightly, as did his tone. "I can't help you." He shook his head. "I don't know anything about your dad's criminal activities." Then he glared pointedly at Kris. "And I don't appreciate the cops or anyone else implying otherwise."

The man appeared to be holding back so much rage. And yet Kris kept an easy stance and neutral expression. He didn't look intimidated, nor did he appear compelled to push back equally hard and prove to Brendan how tough he was. Monica found his self-control admirable. It probably made him a good cop, a good soldier back in the day, and a good dad now.

"When's the last time you talked to Hunter Larson?" Kris asked.

Brendan made a scoffing sound. "Years ago. After his family moved down to Reno, he graduated from college, and not long after that he started making big money. He came back for a visit to show off. It was obnoxious and unappreciated." He looked away for a moment and then turned back to Kris. "We were friends in high school. The friendship ended five or six years later."

"Do you have any idea where my dad would have put something if he wanted to hide it here in Cedar Lodge?" Monica felt a little ridiculous for asking at this point, since it was clear her dad and Brendan hadn't been anything like confidants for a long time, but since the opportunity was here, she voiced the question.

"I do not," Brendan said.

She didn't realize she'd actually gotten her hopes up until she felt the weight of disappointment with his answer.

"It's past business hours," Brendan said, finally uncrossing his arms. "I've got work to finish before I close up, and I'd like to get to it."

"Of course," Monica said. "Thank you for your time."

"If you happen to remember anything later that might help us find information Hunter Larson has stashed somewhere in Cedar Lodge, please give me a call." Kris took a business card from the front pocket of his uniform and held it out. Brendan glared at him for a moment before finally taking it.

Monica wondered if the mechanic had something against cops.

"Another dead end," she muttered after they'd gotten back into the patrol car. "He obviously doesn't know anything about my dad and his criminal issues."

"He might not," Kris said, starting up the car's engine. "It could also be that he knows something about your dad's shady past—even where he might have hidden important information—but he's afraid to talk about it. Boyd Sierra Associates are a dangerous bunch. I can understand him not wanting to cross them. Or him wanting to make certain there's no reason for them to think that he's crossed them. It's a small town, and word gets around."

Kris pulled out onto the road. "Tomorrow I should have time to do a deeper background check on him at the station. I spent most of the day today on patrol and got back barely in time for the meeting. Maybe he's had prior run-ins with the police. I've never interacted with him, but that doesn't mean some other cop hasn't."

"He reminded me of the man who attacked me inside the cabin," Monica said.

Kris gave her a sharp look. "Really?"

"I don't think it's him, though. His voice sounded different."

"The police department has been operating under the assumption that Boyd Sierra might have hired local thugs to do their dirty work." He nodded to himself. "I'll definitely take a closer look at Brendan."

Monica considered what he'd said. Was she mistaken? Could Brendan have been one of the assailants at the cabin? Or even involved in the other assaults? She hadn't gotten a clear look at the attackers at the cabin or when they were coming after her with the car behind the thrift shop. Kris had already told her he hadn't been able to see the faces of the thugs driving the car or van behind the store, either.

The drive back to the ranch was quiet, but Monica felt anxious and jittery the whole way. She rubbed the side of her head, frustrated as she tried again to take her mind back to that prison visit with her dad.

"If only I could remember what Dad told me," she muttered as Kris made the turn onto the ranch driveway. "The more I think about it, the more it seems like I remember the two of us talking about *people* rather than *objects* as we sat together in the prison visiting room." Could he have been telling her about a person rather than hidden documentation? "Perhaps I've been searching for the wrong thing all along."

As had happened so many times before, when she tried to focus on the conversation, the memory or thought or imagining or whatever it was seemed to just fade away. It was so frustrating that her dad was still not allowed to receive visits or phone calls because of the fight he'd gotten into.

Ahead, warm light spilled from several windows of the rambling Volker ranch house, giving it a welcoming appeal.

"If you're starting to recall that you and your dad were talking about people rather than physical items, that's making headway. After you get some food in you and a little rest, maybe your memory will become clearer." Kris parked near the front door of the house. He climbed out of the vehicle and strode around to stand close to Monica as she got out, and they walked the short distance to the porch.

"I saw you driving up on the security camera," Pete said from the foyer once they'd stepped inside. A sleepy-looking Betty sat beside him, thumping her tail lightly on the floor. "Everything go okay?"

"For the most part," Kris answered.

"Well, your mom left you two some dinner in the oven. It's getting late for us, so we're about ready to turn in for the night. Holler if you need anything."

Pete ambled down the long hallway, Betty at his heels, and Kris and Monica moved toward the kitchen.

"You sit down," Kris said, pulling out a chair at the dining table for Monica. "I'll have this ready in a minute."

He grabbed a set of pot holders, took the shepherd's pie out of the oven, and set it on the stove top, then reached for plates in the cupboard.

Monica went to see if there was the usual iced tea or lemonade in the refrigerator. Sitting at the table and being waited on by Kris after all he'd done for her didn't seem right. Three days ago, they hadn't even known each other. She shook her head. It was hard to believe it had only been three days.

She'd filled a couple of glasses with ice cubes and was pouring in the tea when she heard a strange buzzing sound. She looked up, focusing on the noise, trying to figure out what it was. It kind of sounded like a car engine now, but it wasn't coming from the direction of the driveway.

She turned to Kris, and by his unmoving stance and the expression of concentration on his face, she knew he heard it, too. "What could that be?" she asked. "Somebody on an ATV cutting across the pasture, maybe?" Though the sound didn't seem to be coming from that direction, either.

Kris darted to the wall and hit the switch to kill the kitchen lights, hiding them in darkness. Then he hurried to the kitchen window, pushed the blinds aside and looked outside.

Boom!

It was both a roar and a hideous crushing sound, combined with an impact that shook the house to its foundation.

Kris launched himself atop Monica, taking them both to the floor as a hot cloud of wood and concrete debris shot through the still-shuddering house.

NINE

The dust slowly began to settle, and after a moment the air Monica drew into her lungs felt cleaner.

Kris remained propped over her, his arms forming a protective cage around her head.

"Are you okay?" she asked, ending her question with a slight cough.

"Yeah." He adjusted his position so he could look directly at her. "How about you?"

"I'm okay, too." She nodded, grateful to be alive and thankful that she had lived through another potentially deadly attack. Because she was reasonably sure whatever just happened—whatever it turned out to be—was somehow one more attempt on her life.

After a moment, she realized she was grasping Kris's muscular biceps, and she didn't want to let go. Not just yet. Despite the uncertainty of what had just happened, she wanted to rest for a few seconds in the feeling of being safe despite the obvious danger all around. In the feeling of having someone care enough to make her feel like she was someone important.

Was she truly important to him personally? Or was she important in the sense that he was sworn to protect all the citizens of his town? She wanted to believe she already knew. That she'd seen the signs he was interested in her. But she'd misinterpreted situations before. She'd certainly been fooled by her own father when he presented himself as a regular mild-mannered accountant.

She was being ridiculous. Debris still settled around them. There were things going on that were more important than the ridiculous stirrings of romantic hope in her heart.

And then Kris leaned down and tenderly brushed his lips across her forehead.

Her breath caught in her throat. And in the next moment, her entire body relaxed.

Such a small gesture, but a fortifying one. The fear and temptation of falling into hopelessness that had dogged her since the initial attack at the cabin felt as if they had been chased away. At least for the span of a few steady heartbeats, as she turned her attention toward focusing her thoughts.

After a lingering hesitation where they shared a locked gaze, Kris pushed himself up to his feet and then held out his hand, helping Monica get up, too.

"Kris! Monica!" Pete, flashlight in hand, made his way down the hall with Betty and Pepper beside him.

Jill followed, carrying her phone, and already talking to a 9-1-1 operator.

"We're all right," Kris called out. "How about you?"

His dad nodded as he stepped into the kitchen. "We're good."

Kris grabbed his gun from the police utility belt he'd set aside when they'd arrived at the house, and then took Monica's hand as they walked out to the darkened living room. Lights were on in the southern end of the building, but the power was out in the half of the house closer to the point of the explosion.

A light haze of dusty debris still snaked through the air, smelling of concrete and dirt. And something else.

"I smell gasoline," Monica said as she walked cautiously with Kris toward the site of the odd explosion, which was still out of sight. It seemed to be near the family room.

"You feel that draft?" Pete asked. "Windows are broken at the very least."

Monica spotted an orange flicker of light at the end of the hallway. "Something's burning."

Pete shoved his flashlight at Monica and then quickly stepped through the bathroom door beside them, grabbing a small garbage can. He emptied it onto the floor and then started filling it with water.

Meanwhile, after a glance upward to make sure the ceiling was stable, Kris and Monica continued cautiously forward. The floor became more thickly strewn with chunks of wood and drywall. They stepped over part of a lamp and a cushion from one of the family room easy chairs. Still feeling jarred but also curious, Monica stayed beside Kris. The sound of the explosion hadn't been at all like the explosion at the trailer. And the smell in the aftermath of the event was different.

Pete caught up with them just as they entered the family room.

Moderate-sized flames snaked along the wall with the most structural damage, casting shifting light around the otherwise darkened room. There were holes in the wall and snapped beams at the juncture of the wall and the ceiling. Dirt and debris, tree branches and rocks, were strewn across the room.

Pete doused the fire and then hurried back for more water.

"I'm no expert on explosives," Monica said quietly. "But something about this just seems… *off*." Goose bumps rippled across the surface of her skin at the sight of the creepy scene in front of her.

Jill aimed her phone flashlight above the smoking fire until it settled on an object punched into the wall halfway between the floor and the ceiling. It was black and circular.

"A tire?" Monica said. And then, just above it, she spotted something curved and metallic. Her brain struggled to put the pieces together into an idea that made sense. Because it couldn't be what she thought it was. "Is that part of a *car*?" That wasn't possible. She shook her head. "It's too far off the ground for someone to have rammed it into the house."

A voice crackled through Jill's phone. She turned off the flashlight function and put the phone up to her ear. "Emergency response is about eight minutes out," she said.

"I'm going to go take a look outside," Kris said.

Monica reached for his arm. "Shouldn't we stay here?"

"It could be that whoever did this plans to bust in, assuming we're injured or addled, and try to finish us off. I'd rather get in the way of that if I can."

Such a hard lesson Monica had learned over the last few days: sometimes there was no safe option.

"Your mom and I will grab a couple of rifles out of the gun safe and go out with you," Pete said.

They all started back toward the other end of the house, with Kris heading to the kitchen door leading to the side yard rather than the main front entrance.

"Might be better if you stay inside," he said to Monica. "You're the one they're after."

She thought back to her desperate fight with the thug at the Bennett cabin. There was no way she wanted to find herself in that kind of situation again. "I'm staying with you."

He glanced at her, and she was relieved when he didn't argue.

"Stay back." Kris grabbed his police radio and then opened the door, initially remaining behind it and using it as a barricade before moving aside to have a better look around. He cocked his head slightly as if listening. Monica, too, listened closely. For footsteps, or voices, or the sound of someone firing a gun.

Jill and Pete appeared, weapons in hand, and the two of them plus Kris made a quick plan for them to look for bad guys, circling the house as efficiently as possible.

Kris was out the door first, head on a swivel as he continually surveyed his surroundings, staying close to the building as he moved toward the right.

His parents stepped outside. Using equal caution, they headed left.

Monica went with Kris, and as they rounded the end of the house, she finally saw for certain that the *explosion* wasn't an explosion so much as an impact.

The bizarre image of a car actually jammed partway through the house, rear wheels on the ground holding it in place at an odd angle, created the unreal image that someone had actually tried to drive up the exterior wall.

"What am I seeing?" Monica whispered. "How could this have happened?" She was stunned and terrified at the same time.

Kris glanced up at the mountain ridge looming above the house and then at the surrounding snapped tree branches and torn-up grass. "I think someone drove off the fire road on the ridge. This thing didn't just tumble over the edge like it possibly could have in an accident. It had to be going fast and would have shot through the air like a bullet."

"You think someone was actually intending to drive off the ridge and crash onto the house?" Monica could barely believe she was saying those words. It was an unfathomable situation.

"Yes." Kris gestured toward the car embedded in the side of the house. "I'm going to see if the driver survived."

Monica heard approaching sirens.

Stepping cautiously around the precariously balanced vehicle, Kris moved to a spot where he could see part of the cracked windshield. He pulled out his phone and flicked on the flashlight app. "I don't see anyone in there," he called out to Monica after a moment. He continued to peer into the other windows. "I don't see blood. I don't see any sign of anyone."

He keyed his radio and informed dispatch of the situation.

Still overwhelmed, Monica shook her head. "Did the criminals think the car would actually land on me and kill me?"

"Maybe." Kris shrugged. "Or it could be they hoped to get us all running outside, disoriented and unarmed, and then they could pick you off from a distance with a rifle. Or it could be they just hope to get you out of the house permanently and back on the run so it's easier for them to get to you."

His parents approached from the other side of the house. "All clear," his mom reported.

"Nobody in the car. I'm going to guess that whoever did this put a weight on the gas pedal, popped it into gear, and let it go over the edge. There's probably a more sophisticated way to make it happen if you know what you're doing."

"Well, I obviously *do* have to leave now," Monica said, feeling horrible about what she'd put this family through by staying here.

Bam!

The crack of a rifle shot echoed from the ridgetop, followed by several more shots.

Kris grabbed Monica and pulled her around to the side of the house not facing the ridge. His parents were right behind them.

He keyed his radio. "Shots fired on us at the Volker ranch from Fire Road Thirty-Two!"

"Copy. I'm almost to the ranch." The immediate response, with the sound of a siren in the background, sounded like Kris's friend Dylan rather than an emergency dispatcher. "Dispatch, show Deputy Ruiz responding to shots fired. I'm heading for the ridge."

A second deputy confirmed that she'd respond to the ridge location, as well.

There were no subsequent shots fired, and as the minutes ticked by, Monica hoped they'd finally caught a break in the case and the shooter had been captured.

But when Ruiz finally checked in again, it was to report that he and the other deputy had not come across anyone, so the shooter was still at large.

* * *

The following morning, Kris paused from hammering a sheet of plywood into place to take a lingering look around the ranch property and the friends and neighbors who had shown up to help with repairs to the house. *Thank You, Lord.* Last night's horrible event could have been so much worse. He was especially grateful that he'd sent Roy to stay with Angie's parents when Monica first moved in.

He glanced over at Monica, on the porch near the doorway and hopefully out of range of any potential shooter. Penny the calico cat sat beside her, licking her paw and then wiping her face.

The car that had been partially embedded in the house was now at the police impound yard, where it would be swept for evidence. The cable from a winch on a heavy-duty wildlands fire truck had been attached to the sedan and then tightened until it pulled the vehicle to the ground. Kris had quickly confirmed that no one was inside the vehicle. Of course, like the other vehicles used by the attackers, it had been reported stolen.

Kris and Monica had gone with Chief Ellis to take a look at the spot on the fire road where the car had gone over. Tire tracks and footprints were visible in the dirt where the attackers had taken advantage of a small gap between the trees to turn the vehicle into an aimed projectile. If that naturally formed gap had been just a little bit farther to the south, the falling car could have landed in the middle of the house or at the end near the bedrooms, and the outcome could have been much, much worse.

The county roadworks department had already moved a boulder into place so the same insane tactic couldn't be tried twice. The county sheriff had committed to having his deputies patrol that stretch of fire road on a regular basis for at least the next few days. Still, Kris was aware that this didn't necessarily make Monica completely safe. These attackers had proven they would do anything to get to her. Including things Kris could never imagine.

Kris's mom walked by him carrying a couple of wooden planks, and she offered him a tired smile. The chief had left a cop stationed outside the ranch house last night while Monica and the Volkers tried to sleep, but it was fairly evident that none of them had gotten much rest.

Kris glanced at Monica again. It seemed like she had been avoiding him all morning. Was she understandably scared after last night's attack? Or was it something else?

Could she be unhappy about him kissing her on her forehead? In the moment, he'd been so glad she was alive. But had it made things weird between them? Had he overstepped his bounds?

He put down his hammer and walked over to her. He would apologize if he needed to. Maybe he should offer her a half truth and explain how he'd simply given in to an impulse of the moment. He didn't need to admit he'd been compelled by something more and that a feeling of concern for her had combined with attraction leading to a gesture he now realized was completely out of line.

"I need to get out of here," she said as he approached her on the porch.

She'd mentioned something about leaving last night, and Kris had hoped she'd forgotten about it. He pushed aside a sinking sensation, determined to come across as calm and reasonable despite the fear that she would leave.

"Let's just give it some time before you decide what to do next. I know you're shaken up. We all are." Kris had been through some rough situations in the military and as a cop. As a civilian and the direct target of so much violence, he could only imagine how Monica felt.

She shook her head, and the light breeze blew tendrils of wavy blond hair in front of her face. "How can I stay? Look what happened to your parents' house. Look at how I've put people in danger."

"You aren't to blame for any of this. And you deserve to be protected."

Kris reached out to brush the strands of hair aside and tuck them behind her ear.

She didn't seem to mind the gesture, as unshed tears shimmered in her eyes. The soft feel of her skin made him feel even more protective, and he let his fingertips linger on her cheek for a moment before finally dropping his hand. He couldn't help noticing the flush of color in her cheeks and wondered if his cheeks had been reddened by a rush of emotion, too.

She held his gaze for a moment, then shifted it away. But she didn't step back. And Kris didn't move away from her, either.

There truly was something between them. He knew it now. It wasn't just him. Where he wanted it to go, he still wasn't sure.

Monica's phone chimed, and she slid it out of her pocket to look at the screen. "It's Ryan Fergus. Video call."

She tapped the screen, and Kris stepped beside her. He found himself looking at a fit, older gentleman wearing a dark blue polo shirt with the Elk Ridge Resort logo stitched onto it.

"You're all right," Ryan said. "I wanted to see for myself."

"I'm okay," Monica said before offering a nervous laugh. "They keep trying to kill me, and I keep surviving."

"I've been off my phone most of the morning,

and I just now saw on the local news site what happened. Is there anything I can do to help? Do you need me to find a safe place for you to stay here at the resort?"

Kris watched Ryan's glance shift toward him a couple of times.

"I don't need that right now, but I might eventually," Monica said.

"I'm still doing what I can to think of people your dad mentioned who might know something useful and be able to help you out. Or who might have had a grudge against him, for that matter."

"Where were you last night about eight o'clock?" Kris asked. That was roughly the time of the attack.

Ryan drew his head back, rapidly blinking in apparent surprise while Monica looked at Kris from the corner of her eye.

"Ryan is helping me," she said to Kris in a patient, teacher-like tone. "If he wanted to hurt me, he would have had the chance when I walked right up to him at the resort."

Maybe so. But Kris was not taking any chances. And anyone who followed true crime stories, let alone who actually fought crime, had heard of *helpful* people who were actually in on the crime.

"This is Officer Kris Volker," Monica said to Ryan.

"I went out for a late dinner with a couple of friends last night," Ryan finally said, sounding as if he were insulted. "After we ate, we moved to the restaurant lounge to have an after-dinner drink and chat for a while. We met there at seven thirty and stayed a couple of hours."

After Kris got the name of the restaurant, he pulled out his phone and texted a message to Chief Ellis with the specifics, asking if he would have someone check out Ryan's alibi. By the time he hit Send, Monica had ended her conversation with Ryan, and she turned to him. "I hope he doesn't take offense and stop offering assistance. I need all the help I can get."

"If he really was where he said he was, he shouldn't have a problem with the question. Your life is in danger. If he's annoyed, then he obviously isn't much of a friend."

"I don't know that I'd exactly describe him as a friend," Monica said thoughtfully.

The sound of a truck rumbling up the driveway caught Kris's attention. He stepped to where he had a better view and spotted a well-worn green pickup truck with a camper shell on the back moving toward the house. A smile crossed his lips.

"Who is it?" Monica asked, turning to get a clearer look.

"It's Cole. You've met him."

"Oh, the paramedic?"

Kris nodded.

They walked toward the truck as Cole parked it and got out. "Wouldn't want you to work too hard, so I came to help," the medic called out teasingly as a greeting while walking up to Kris and Monica.

"You're just here because you have no social life," Kris shot back with a grin.

"Just not one I tell you about." Cole offered Monica a smile before his expression turned serious. "I am so sorry these terrible things keep happening to you. I was on the other side of the county working a traffic accident when the call about the attack last night came through, so I couldn't respond." He glanced over at Kris's parents, who were standing together by the side of the house, talking. "I'm glad everybody's okay."

"Could have been worse."

"Yeah, and with that in mind…" He gestured toward his truck. "I plan to be out here whenever I'm not working as long as Monica is staying here. I'll sleep in the camper."

Touched by the offer and more than willing to accept his help, Kris scoffed. "Don't be ridiculous. You can sleep in the stable with the horses."

"What?" Monica demanded.

"No, seriously, stay in the bunkhouse. You know how nice it is."

"Dylan's going to stay in there. When he's off shift with the sheriff's department, he'll be here, too."

Kris felt a lump of emotion in his throat. He was blessed to have such good friends.

Knowing that an effusive offer of thanks would only make Cole uncomfortable, Kris cleared his throat and said, "Just don't eat us out of house and home while you're here."

Cole hitched the corner of his mouth up in a half smile. "I'm not making any promises."

The two men exchanged manly thumps on the upper arm, which earned them an eye roll from Monica. After that, Cole turned and walked toward a work crew who were tearing out sections of the damaged wall to prep it for repair.

"Good friends are worth so much," Monica said quietly. "After my dad got arrested, I learned I didn't have as many as I'd thought I did. But the ones who were willing to stand by me in the worst of it have added a lot to my life." She sighed heavily. "Shelly Bennett offered me the use of her family cabin because she wanted to help, and it got set on fire. And now, look at the damage to your house. I don't want my friends to suffer because someone is coming after me."

Kris opened his mouth to say something that would make her agree to stay, though he had no idea what it should be. But he was interrupted when Monica's phone chimed again.

"It's a text from Esmeralda. She says someone told her that my dad liked to hang out at the Wind Ridge golf course when he was in town." She looked up at Kris. "I'd forgotten about that. He did like to play golf in the spring and summer when the weather was good."

She turned back to the screen. "Some friend of Esmeralda's told her they saw Dad hanging out in the clubhouse there a lot. Sometimes with my mom and sometimes alone. He appeared to have the same regular group of friends."

"I don't suppose you'll let me go ask around there and see if I can learn anything while you stay here?"

Monica gave him a direct look. "I want to be safe, obviously. But hiding won't solve anything, and it will likely slow down my efforts. As I've mentioned before, there are details that might not be meaningful to you, but if I heard them, they'd be meaningful to me. Even if your department catches the thugs, I still have to find evidence to prove to my mom that Archer is a criminal before she marries him. And that same information might help take down the entire Boyd Sierra Associates crime syndicate or at least do some serious damage. They're into extortion, drug dealing, all kinds of things. Imagine the potential for misery that could be stopped if they were destroyed. Or at least weakened."

"True. All right, we'll go to the golf course. Maybe there's a bartender or a restaurant manager we can talk to who remembers something about your dad." They walked into the house. "You ever thought of a future career as a detective?" Kris asked.

Monica shrugged. "Right now, when it comes to looking toward the future, I don't have any specific plans. I would be grateful to just stay alive."

TEN

The golf course on the western end of town offered a gorgeous view of the Meadowlark River.

Monica was getting a good look at the scenery because, like Kris, she was glancing around constantly to see if they were being followed. Vigilance had become second nature to her since the cabin attack, and she wondered if it would be a habit that continued through the rest of her life. The possibility that she might need to watch her back forever was chilling.

They were riding in one of the ranch trucks. Kris was concerned that the attackers might be looking for a patrol vehicle to find Monica, so they were traveling discreetly in the old pickup. He was also dressed in regular clothes instead of his uniform because he wanted to keep a lower profile. For all they knew, the bad guys had been watching them from the moment they left ranch property, but they could still do their best to be as safe as possible.

Kris's handheld police radio lay on the bench seat between them, crackling with various transmissions between officers and the town's emergency dispatch center. Everything sounded routine and relatively quiet.

"I came out here a few times as a kid," Monica said as they drew closer to the sprawling golf course. A light breeze sent a spray of water from a fountain in the middle of a water hazard across the bright green grass.

Kris turned into the parking lot and found a space near the portico. After the obligatory few moments looking around to see if they'd been followed, they got out and walked through the smoked-glass doors into the foyer and then veered off toward the restaurant with its adjoining lounge.

The serving table for the breakfast buffet was being disassembled, and it was too early for the lunch crowd. The facility with its large windows, dark wood paneling, and plush maroon carpeting was nearly empty except for a couple of patrons sipping from coffee mugs at a table near the door to the back patio.

A man behind the bar with a clipboard appeared to be taking inventory of the bottles stored on the shelves.

"Looks like he's a manager of some sort," Monica commented. "Maybe he's been employed here long enough to know the regulars, and he's noticed something."

"Worth a shot," Kris said, and they headed toward him.

"Good morning," Kris called out as they approached the man.

Monica reminded herself to smile. Tension had worn her nerves thin, and she was certain her feeling of anxious desperation showed on her face. She couldn't help wondering if she'd already interacted with someone who had useful information, but they were afraid to speak up. If she wanted people to help, she needed to seem somewhat friendly and approachable. She was asking people to stick their necks out, possibly putting themselves in danger if they gave her information in any way related to Boyd Sierra Associates. It was a lot to ask. Being pleasant while she asked for help was the least she could do.

The lounge employee, dressed in black slacks and a dress shirt, turned to offer them a polite, professional smile. "Good morning." A small brass-colored name tag declared him Daniel, and beneath it was written Food and Beverage Services Manager. "May I get you something to drink?"

"Actually, we'd just like to talk to you for a minute," Monica said.

Daniel nodded cautiously. "Sure."

"Have you worked here for a while?" she asked.

"Oh, yeah, I started bussing tables on weekends when I was still in high school." He offered a small smile. "And as you can see, that was a few years ago."

Monica figured he was about forty years old, give or take.

"Good." She nodded, still striving to appear upbeat. "I was hoping to ask you some questions about a customer who's been a seasonal visitor in the past. It's my dad, actually." She pulled out her phone, tapped on a photo and held it up.

Daniel leaned across the bar to have a look. As his gaze went to the picture, Monica said, "His name is Hunter Larson."

Daniel's smile faltered.

"You know who he is," Monica said. It was a statement, not a question.

"Yeah, sure," Daniel said hesitantly. He appeared uncomfortable and then glanced briskly around the lounge and toward the dining room as if looking for an excuse to walk away.

"You know about his criminal conviction," Monica said, figuring there was no point in beating around the bush.

"A couple of our guests were talking about it once and I couldn't help overhearing some of their conversation."

"I understand he liked to hang out with the

same group of friends when he came out to play a few rounds, and they'd relax together here afterward. Could you tell me who those friends were?"

Daniel grabbed a bar towel and began rubbing it on a glass that already looked dry. "Why are you asking?"

"I'm trying to track down some information," she said, quickly thinking of how she could state her case as succinctly as possible. "People's lives are at stake. I believe one or more of my dad's associates know things that could help me and that possibly should be shared with the authorities. I just want to talk to them. It seems likely that they're still members here."

He shook his head. "Sorry, but I can't help you."

"Can't or won't?" Kris asked.

Daniel glanced at him. "You're a police officer. I've seen you before."

Kris nodded. "I am. And if you pay attention to the news, you know there are some dangerous people active in town right now. Any information you could give us would be a big help."

"I mind my own business," Daniel said with a tone of finality. "There's no way I'm crossing organized crime. Not even with something as simple as telling you who your dad hung out with when he was here. I have no idea who is

connected to what, and I don't want to get involved. Now, I'm happy to get you something to
eat or drink, but that's it."

Monica was frustrated, but she couldn't force
the man to give them an answer.

Kris took out a business card and set it on the
counter. "In case you change your mind or think
of something."

Back outside, Monica looked up at the vibrant
blue sky overhead. Such a beautiful day, such a
gorgeous setting. People going about their normal lives all around her. And yet here she was,
the target of murderers and getting nowhere in
her efforts to set things to rights in her life and
get very bad guys sent to jail.

"How do you do it?" She turned to Kris,
who was focused on their surroundings as they
walked to the truck.

"I pray a lot. I do the best I can. I accept that
ultimately I am not in control," he answered
without hesitation. He hadn't needed her to
explain what she meant, and it seemed like a
confirmation of her feeling that they'd come to
understand each other in a ridiculously short
amount of time. The basis of that seemed to be
that they had faith in common. But there was
something more specific to each of them, too.
Something that just felt *right*—at least to Monica—when they were together.

She felt comfortable with him. His calmness and strength were reassuring. Having a dad who turned out to be secretly committing white-collar crimes had undermined her trust in people in general. But seeing Kris with his family and friends and coworkers showed her that he truly was the kind of man he presented himself to be. Some people, like him, were trustworthy.

He didn't deserve to have his world turned sideways by a woman whose future was uncertain and who brought danger wherever she went.

Kris had this meaningful life where he was of service to his community. He had an adorable son and a lovely family. Even if things were to move forward between the two of them, how could Monica possibly fit into his life without creating a rift? He was a lawman, and she was the daughter of a dishonest mob accountant. Her dad had come to faith, and she was grateful for that. But he remained accountable for his actions. And her name was associated with his. How could she tarnish the name of Officer Kris Volker?

What were the chances of her getting a teaching job in a town where people might know about her dad? There were undoubtedly more of them who were aware of his exploits since the attacks on Monica had made it into the local news. And what if all her efforts failed and nothing substantial happened to the Boyd Sierra syndicate? What if they carried a grudge against Monica and anyone close to her for the rest of her life?

Kris was kind and brave, and his family was supportive and generous. How could she bring trouble to them? What kind of thank-you was that?

It would be selfish and self-centered. It was something she wouldn't do. Painful as it was, sad as it was, she needed to rein in her emotions and be more controlled in her responses to Kris's attention.

"I want to stop by the police station before we go back to the ranch," Kris said while they were still in the parking lot. A moment later his phone chimed, and he checked it. "Here's some good news for you. Your friend Ryan's alibi checks out. He was at the restaurant when he said he was. Witnesses confirm it, and there's security video footage of him."

"I'm glad to hear it." It was good news. But given the weight of the thoughts on her mind, she didn't exactly feel happy.

"Ryan seems pretty concerned about the guy who was working at the resort when you went up there."

"Jason Mulhern." In her mind, Monica pictured the paving company truck she'd seen and the man she'd almost bumped into. She assumed that had been Jason.

"Talking to him should be our next step." He tapped some information into his cell phone. "Looks like Mulhern's shop isn't far from downtown. Let's stop by and see what he has to say on our way back to the ranch from the police station." He put aside the phone and drove out of the parking lot.

"Brendan was pretty hostile when we went to talk to him last night," Monica said as they rode down the road. "It seemed like he felt as if Dad had betrayed their friendship, but maybe it was something more. Or maybe he's just an angry person all the time." She shrugged. "It's hard to imagine him getting angry and sending a car off a ridge onto your house. That seems far-fetched. But I do wonder if he's somehow connected to the attacks on me. He was the right size for the attacker inside the cabin, but since his voice was different I just don't think he was that guy." She shook her head. "But maybe I'm wrong. Maybe I'm misremembering, and he is one of the attackers. He seemed over-the-top defensive. What do you think?"

"Given all that's happened, I think we should stay suspicious of everyone. You coming back to town and going around with a cop asking questions is bound to stir up a few secrets and fears.

I'm hoping it will awaken somebody's guilty conscience and prod them to do the right thing. That does happen, but unfortunately it takes time. Maybe we'll start to get some results for our efforts soon."

"I hope so. I don't have time to waste." Not to mention that she was exhausted by the constant fear weighing her down.

They approached a railroad crossing as the gates dropped down in front of them. Kris stopped and shifted the truck into Park. He glanced in the rearview mirror, did a double take, and then yelled, "Get down!" He lunged across the bench seat, pressing Monica's head down and protecting it with his own body as bullets slammed into the cab's rear window and pounded into the back of the truck.

"We can't move. We're boxed in!" Monica cried out as the shots kept coming. "The train is in front of us, and the shooter is behind us."

"We *have* to move." Kris sat back up behind the steering wheel while keeping his head ducked as much as possible.

They were pinned in by a concrete traffic barrier on one side that made it impossible to do a U-turn and the brick exterior of an industrial building on the other.

"How can we get away? Which direction can we go?" Monica raised her head slightly to peer into her side mirror, where she saw a heavy SUV behind them. She could see the open passenger door, with a gunman crouched behind it, firing through the gap. He paused and looked as though he was getting ready to move forward. Possibly to shoot Monica point-blank through the side window. And then shoot Kris, too.

She knew Kris had a gun, but she could see that the interior of the besieged truck was not a good place to set up some kind of defensive position. Surrounded by glass, and with Monica unarmed, they were too vulnerable.

"Hang on!" Kris slammed the truck into gear and made a right turn so sharp the truck initially struggled to move forward. The vehicle rocked and swayed as he drove off the pavement, around the crossing gates, and onto the dusty right-of-way alongside the rail line.

They raced beside the train. Loud clanks and squeals on the railroad cars launched a frightening assault on Monica's ears. It was accompanied by a deep rumbling vibration that she not only heard but also felt in her gut.

"Call it in on my radio!"

The truck stirred up dust that swirled around them as the truck rattled across the rutted hard-packed dirt.

Bang! Bang!

The assailants had followed them!

More shots slammed into the back of the truck's cab. Monica took a quick look in the side mirror and saw the SUV was now frighteningly close on their tail.

She reached for the radio, but it wasn't there. Feeling a flare of panic that sent a grip of fear through her whole body, she looked around and then slid down to the floorboard, where she finally discovered it had slipped under her side of the seat.

"Key it and say *shots fired*," Kris called to her as he fought with the jerking steering wheel on the rough stretch of dirt that wasn't even really a road. "Tell them you're with Officer Volker."

She followed his directions.

"Copy shots fired," a voice on the radio responded. "All units clear the channel. What is your location?"

What *was* their location? What should she say? That they were gunning it alongside a train near the golf course? She had no idea of the nearby street names.

"East of Lampson Street on the southern side of the railroad right-of-way, heading east toward Sunrise Avenue," Kris said in a tone so calm and controlled that Monica actually found it eerie.

Squeezing her eyes shut to help her concentrate, she repeated the words, hearing the shakiness in her voice, which vibrated with every dip and bump along the ground not meant for high-speed driving.

At Kris's prompting, she added a description of the vehicle pursuing them and mentioned there were two shooters.

After that, Monica could hear the dispatcher speaking with police units checking in their estimated response time, but she was more focused on keeping her balance as Kris made another sharp right turn, this time onto the first actual paved street they came to.

"Tell them we're southbound on Sunrise Avenue now."

She wanted to do what he said, but fear had a grip on her so tight she could barely think, let alone move. Her breath felt locked in her chest, and all she could do was stare straight ahead with her hands braced against the dashboard so she'd be ready if he took another sharp turn.

"We'll shake them," Kris said with only a slight hint of concern in his voice. "Just hang on for a little while longer."

This whole race to stay ahead of the shooters felt like deadly, random chaos to Monica. But Kris obviously knew how to deal with it, and his even-tempered focus helped settle her emotions once again. She took a breath and said, "Southbound on Sunrise," into the radio.

They were in an industrial part of town, with

brick warehouses and repair garages and light manufacturing businesses.

Kris made a sudden turn into a narrow alley between two warehouses, his truck barely fitting between the oversized blue trash cans pressed against the outer walls of the buildings. Almost immediately after that, he took a turn into another narrow alley before coming to a stop, eyes glued on his rearview mirror.

Without the roar of the train beside them or the whine of the pickup's engine, Monica was finally able to hear emergency sirens.

"What should I tell them now?" she asked, radio near her face, her voice not much more than a whisper. "How do I describe where we are?"

He shook his head. "We don't. We hope and pray the shooters didn't see us make the first turn, or the turn after that. They might have a scanner and be listening to police traffic, so we don't want to say specifically where we are. We had to use the radio to coordinate a response with the other cops, but now we can use a phone so we don't inadvertently tell the thugs how to find us."

Bang! Bang!

Just as he finished speaking, they heard shots fired, followed by the sound of brakes squealing and then a car crash. It came from the direction of where they would have been if Kris hadn't turned.

The sound of sirens grew increasingly loud, and it sounded like the cops sped past the alley entrance Kris had turned into as they raced by in pursuit of the assailants.

The sirens wailed in place for a few moments, and then they were silenced.

Radio traffic commenced with an officer reporting the vehicle they'd been pursuing had crashed, two suspects had bailed on foot, and the officers were in pursuit.

The dispatcher responded that the sheriff's department K-9 team was on the way.

Kris drove through the alley until they reached the street and could see the intersection where the SUV had crashed against a light pole. The front doors were hanging open.

Two patrol units were parked on scene, and an officer was on the sidewalk talking to a citizen who gestured as if they were describing everything they'd witnessed.

"Should we stay and help?" Monica asked.

Kris shook his head. "What we need to do is get you out of here. The criminals could double back on foot and come after you if they know you're nearby. They may not be far away. They might even be watching to see if we show up on the scene."

He grabbed his cell and placed a call to dispatch to let them know that he and Monica would be heading to the police station to give their official statements about what had happened. After he was finished, he pulled out onto the street. The cracked spiderweb of safety glass at the back of the cab allowed air to flow through the small spaces that had actually been blown out by bullets. Bullets that could have killed either one of them.

"You have to wonder how many more times we can survive attacks like this," Monica said wearily.

Kris ran a hand through his bristly, military-cut hair as he exhaled a deep sigh. "As many times as we have to."

"So the only thing we've got on Brendan Stryker, at least on record, is that he's a hot-head and has faced a few assault charges," Kris said, gaze fixed on his computer screen at the police station. "It could be he's committed other crimes and never got caught, but it could also be true that his temper and inability to resist using his fists to solve conflicts are his only problems." He glanced at Monica, who was seated in a chair across from him, and winced inwardly at the sorrowful expression on her face. She was a good person who'd been through so much, and he was compelled to do everything he could to help her. It was probably a good thing that they were still at the police station after giving their reports on the shooting attack. If they were back at the ranch, he might not have been able to avoid the temptation to take her in his arms and try to offer whatever comfort he could.

"Have you found out anything about Mulhern, the guy with the paving company, that shows him criminally active?" Detective Campbell had returned to the police station after hearing about the criminals' attempt to ambush Monica and Kris while they were stopped at the railroad crossing. "None of my informants know anything about the guy."

Kris shook his head. "He does have a criminal record. He broke into a couple of unoccupied homes and stole a few things when he was young. He did his time, and he's no longer under probation, so I can't force him to come in and talk to me. I was going to stop by his paving business this afternoon and ask him a few questions, but given what's just happened, I think it would be best to get Monica back to the ranch."

He glanced at Monica, and braced for an argument that she had no time to waste and would want to talk to Mulhern as soon as possible. But in this instance, she looked at him, exhaustion written on her face and in her slightly slumped posture, and nodded.

The chief strode out of his office, phone to his ear and a tablet in his hand, finishing a conversation and then disconnecting. "The county K-9 team tracked the suspects from the point where they bailed out of their vehicle to a grocery store parking lot four blocks over, where the scent trail stopped."

"What does that mean?" Monica asked. "That they have accomplices in town who picked them up?"

The chief shook his head. "Actually, it looks like they just stole themselves another car. The manager of the grocery store gave the officers access to security video, and they could see perps who generally looked like the assailants breaking into a car and getting away."

"Maybe we should run a check on all known car thieves in town," Kris said. "These guys seem to be very good at that."

"Not a bad idea," Campbell mused. "Does the video footage show us their faces so we can ID them?"

Ellis tapped the screen a couple of times and then set the tablet on Kris's desk so they could have a look. "You can see their builds and get a sense of their heights," he said as the video played. "But they've got sunglasses on and their jacket collars flipped up. There's not enough for facial recognition."

Kris leaned over to watch as the lackluster-quality video played out. "I'd say these are probably the same men who attacked Monica at the Bennett cabin. Which indicates it's likely been the same attackers all along and the Boyd Sierra syndicate hasn't sent multiple killers to Cedar Lodge. That's been my biggest fear."

He turned to Monica, and she nodded. "I agree. I think the slightly shorter and wider guy is the one who grappled with me at the cabin and tried to force me into the fire. The taller guy is the one who was waiting outside."

"We're going to catch them," Chief Ellis said to Monica. "I know you're in a tough situation and that you're likely getting discouraged, but I want you to know this police department supports you. We're not going to give up until we find these criminals. *I* am not going to give up until I've done all I can to support your efforts to uncover the information you believe your dad left for you. Finding it could benefit the whole town. We want these thugs convinced that it's no longer safe for them to engage in any kind of illegal activities in Cedar Lodge, Montana."

Kris reached out to take Monica's hand and gave it a light squeeze.

The look in her eyes when she turned to him,

a glassy-eyed expression of acknowledgment and trust, nearly took his breath away. In his heart, he made a promise to her that he would continue doing all he could to keep her safe and help her protect her family.

She blinked, looked away, and then withdrew her hand from his.

"Going forward, I'm assigning an officer, in addition to Kris, to go with you anytime you leave the Volker family ranch," Ellis said to Monica. "Give me an hour's advance notice, and I'll redirect a cop on patrol to escort you wherever you're going. We're a relatively small department. Given the circumstances, I can justify having Kris assigned to work your case and protect you. I'm afraid I can't justify the cost of a second round-the-clock bodyguard. But I'll do what I can."

"Thank you," Monica said.

"An officer will follow you two back to the Volker ranch as soon as you're ready to go."

Kris's truck would need some windows replaced and holes patched, but he figured on taking care of that later. It was in good enough shape to get them back home.

"Do you have any new leads to follow on this investigation?" Ellis asked. "Beyond talking to Jason Mulhern after you've had time to recover from today's events?"

"No, sir," Kris said. "But we'll find something."

Detective Campbell got to his feet. "My team is still looking for leads, too. I've got another call scheduled tomorrow morning to check in with my federal law enforcement colleagues."

"All right," Chief Ellis said. "Everybody stay alert." He glanced at Kris and said, "Ask whoever is available to follow you home when you're ready to leave." Then he headed back to his office.

Kris turned to Monica. "I'm ready to go now. How about you?"

She nodded.

After finding an officer to escort them, Kris and Monica headed out the door toward the parking lot. They needed to make forward progress on this case soon. Normally quiet Cedar Lodge was starting to feel as dangerous as any combat zone.

ELEVEN

Monica had a robust appetite just hours after she and Kris had nearly been shot to death. She wondered what that said about her. Maybe it meant she was getting used to living on the edge of danger. It was hard to believe her life had turned out like this.

Jill set a casserole dish packed with baked spaghetti on the dining table close to Monica. Her stomach rumbled.

After their return to the ranch, Monica and Kris had given his parents a full report regarding what had happened. Of course everyone was concerned, but at the moment, what more could they do beyond try to stay safe while Monica and Kris tracked down the information Monica was seeking? After the debrief, everyone returned to their routine activities. Jill and Pete had started dinner and declined any offer of help, insisting that Monica and Kris rest. Shortly before mealtime, they'd been joined by Cole and Dylan, who had both just finished their work shifts.

"This feels like old times with you kids here," Jill said.

"Kids?" Kris glanced at Cole and Dylan before dropping his chin and giving his mom a deadpan stare. And then he broke into a wide smile.

He was a man who took dire situations seriously, could talk things out and admit to being worried or afraid. But at some point, he would collect himself and radiate a faith-filled confidence that made Monica feel confident, too. Well, *somewhat* confident.

"You boys will always be kids to your mom," Pete said as he gestured to Monica to help herself to the savory spaghetti in front of her.

She dished up her food, and while waiting for the others, she glanced around the room, her gaze lingering on the rifles propped against the nearby walls. She knew Kris and Dylan were wearing their sidearms. For all she knew, everybody at the table but her was armed. They were enjoying a lighthearted family meal, and yet at the same time, everyone acknowledged that another attack could happen at any moment. Apparently, for the Volker family, huddling together somewhere, overwhelmed with fear, was not an option.

The curtains and blinds around the dining area were closed as a precaution so that no ill-intentioned lurker could see inside the house. Repairs to the damaged section of the home had been partially completed thanks to the help offered by so many people. The Volkers were still awaiting customized items like precisely sized windows and window frames, but eventually the house would look good as new.

"The boys played football together in high school." Jill continued her earlier conversational topic about Kris and his friends as everyone started digging in. "They did junior rodeo. They went hiking and camping and fishing, all that stuff. And man, did they eat us out of house and home when all four of them were here." She turned to Monica. "The fourth musketeer, Henry, works all over the world, and we don't see him much anymore."

Her comment sounded a little wistful to Monica.

Cole, the tall paramedic who Monica had learned was a navy veteran, said, "Henry will come back to town one of these days, and when he does, he'll probably come by here asking for something to eat." He looked down at the huge spoonful of food he'd just scooped up and then glanced up with a guilty expression followed by a grin.

"Don't worry," Jill said, grinning back at him. "I made two casseroles in case we need more. I know who I'm dealing with here."

Dark-haired Dylan turned to his friend and shook his head. "You act like you haven't eaten in days."

Cole shrugged. "I love Mrs. Volker's spaghetti casserole," Cole said. "I always have."

Betty gave a low *woof* from the living room followed by a growl.

Kris, Cole, and Dylan were on their feet in an instant. The others stood, as well.

So much for the appearance of a calm family dinner.

Monica felt the couple of bites of casserole she'd eaten turn to lead in her stomach. Dread settled around her shoulders, giving her a chill. Which direction would the attack come from this time? She followed Betty as the hound moved toward the foyer, seemingly focused on the front door.

"I'll check the security feed." Pete slid his phone out of his pocket and tapped the screen.

Kris was at the dining room window, moving the blind slightly aside to peer out. Cole moved toward the front door, near where Monica was standing, while Dylan took up a position by a living room window.

Betty let out another low bark. Little Pepper stood beside her.

"Looks like it's your police escort," Pete said with his gaze focused on his phone.

It was a cop?

That was strange. They'd had an officer follow them home from the station, but there'd been no plans for him to stay on the property. And there were no other police escorts scheduled to show up at the ranch. Chief Ellis's directions had been that Monica and Kris should call for an officer when they planned to leave the ranch.

What was going on?

Monica walked back to the dining room, where Kris opened the blind a little wider. Monica moved closer to him while staying out of sight. A patrol car rolled slowly up the driveway and then headed past the front entrance and toward the section of the house where the car from the ridge had been partially embedded in the wall.

"Looks like the patrolman is taking a look behind the house," Pete said moments later.

Monica was suddenly aware that fear had tightened her lungs so badly she could barely breathe.

The patrol car came back around.

"I'm going to go talk to the officer," Kris said.

He glanced at Cole, and his friend strode out the front door with him.

Monica stood by the partially open door, muscles taut, peeking and listening. Cole stood on the bottom step, continually scanning their surroundings.

The officer stopped and rolled down his window.

"What's up?" Kris called out, approaching the car.

"We've got officers up on the ridge responding to a vehicle fire. I'm just taking a look around and making sure there's nobody on your property that you didn't invite here."

Goose bumps rippled across the surface of Monica's skin as she imagined Boyd Sierra killers creeping down the mountainside and waiting until the home's occupants were asleep before launching another attack.

"None of the dogs barked until you drove up," Kris said.

"Good sign. At least for the moment."

At least for the moment. That wasn't very comforting.

A voice came across the patrolman's radio. "I found an SUV up here. No plates. Looks like someone tried to set the interior on fire but it fizzled out. I'll check for a vehicle identification number."

"I wonder if that's the SUV the attackers were driving the night of the fire," Monica said loudly enough for Kris to hear.

He glanced at her, pulled his phone out of his pocket, and placed a call. It sounded like he was talking to the officer up on the ridge and asking for a photo of the car. Moments after he ended the call, his phone pinged. He tapped the screen, looked at the picture, and then stepped toward the door to show it to Monica.

The sight still made Monica's skin crawl. "That's their SUV."

Kris nodded. "I think so, too."

"Why would they do this?" Monica asked, still remaining partially hidden by the door at the house's entrance. "Why ditch it and try to set it on fire on that ridge? And why do it now?"

Kris shrugged. "Maybe they planned to send a flaming car rolling down the hill in another attempt to get us all to run outside so they could shoot you. Or maybe they just wanted a fire on the hill to draw attention. To show that they know where you are. To scare you."

If they wanted to scare her, it was working.

And paired with that fear was dread. How many more attacks would be launched at or around this house? How many times would Kris or his family or friends be put into danger because they were close to her?

Things couldn't keep going the way they were. Something had to change. It wasn't enough for her to try to emotionally distance herself from Kris. It was time to put some physical distance between them, too.

Kris exchanged a few more words with the officer, letting him know that he and Monica had recognized the burned vehicle. Then the patrolman drove off.

"Cole and I are going to have a look around," Kris said before he and his friend set off toward the stables and barn.

"If anybody's hiding out in one of the outbuildings, they'll find them." Dylan stepped up to stand beside Monica.

They kept an eye on the men checking the property until they returned. By the time the two longtime friends came back inside, both were wearing serious expressions. They walked into the center of the house where Kris's parents were waiting.

"We didn't see anything notable, but I still think we should make sure someone is awake and keeping an eye on the security cameras throughout the night," Kris said. "We could split it up into short shifts so we can all still function and do our jobs tomorrow."

Everyone nodded in agreement.

They sat back down to finish eating dinner,

but by now, Monica's appetite had drastically diminished. The hard knot in her stomach made it difficult to swallow food, but she did the best she could. With danger all around them, she needed to remain strong and alert.

After dinner, Monica walked up to Kris in the living room, where he'd cast the ranch security feed onto a smart TV on the wall. Jill and Pete were still in the kitchen, talking, while Cole and Dylan had gone to grab the sleeping bags each of them had brought. They'd changed their original plans and were both going to camp out in the ranch house living room instead of Cole staying in his camper and Dylan in the bunkhouse.

"I need to talk to you," Monica said.

Kris turned from the screen. "Sure."

Monica took a deep breath. "Listen, I appreciate everything you have done for me. But I've decided it's time for me to go." She'd pondered it aloud before, but she really meant it now.

Kris stared at her, his face unreadable. So she continued, the words spilling out as she nervously rubbed the stitches on her scalp. "I think I was wrong," she blurted out, tears forming in her eyes because she was scared and sad and frustrated that the pivotal memories of that prison conversation just wouldn't come back. "We haven't gotten anywhere. We haven't found any object or note or key or receipt or anything that could lead us to some clue I thought my dad might have left here. Nobody has come forward with information he entrusted to them."

She brushed away the tears at the corners of her eyes, and then hugged herself, determined to keep going and say what she needed to say. She wouldn't mention how sorry she was to have brought such danger to him and his family, because he was a generous and honorable man who would tell her that her concern wasn't reason enough for her to leave.

When she looked at Kris's face, she was reminded of the sweet image of his little boy. It was unfair to keep father and son apart any longer. It didn't matter that all reports were that Roy was having a wonderful time with his other set of grandparents and the cousins who lived nearby.

She shook her head slightly, doing her best to dismiss feelings she admittedly had for this man and her appreciation of his family. In the scheme of things, what did her feelings matter?

She'd brought danger to Kris's family home. She couldn't possibly risk bringing danger to his son, and Roy needed to come home eventually.

"I want you to stay," Kris said simply.

She straightened her spine and lifted her chin. "I have a reasonable plan. If I can get to the airport without the Boyd Sierra thugs seeing me, I'd have a good head start. I don't have siblings, but I do have cousins in Nevada, and also in California. It might be wiser if I stayed with them. I wouldn't stand out in a densely populated area the way I do in Cedar Lodge." She paused for a moment before continuing. "We haven't gotten anywhere with our investigation, and I'm running out of time to convince my mom that Archer Nolan is part of the mob before she marries him. But maybe, once the prison officials allow my dad to have visitors again, I'll be able to find the proof that will ultimately make her realize Archer's been lying to her. In the meantime, if you hear back from anyone in town who has some information to share, you can let me know."

"I want you to stay," Kris repeated. Only this time, he took a step closer. The expression on his face shifted. It was hard to believe she'd once thought he looked like a typical skeptical cop. His eyes softened with concern. He reached up to rest his fingertips on her cheek. "I want to help you through this. And then I want to see what happens between us afterward."

There wouldn't be any afterward. That was the thing. Boyd Sierra Associates was a strong criminal organization, and if they stayed angry with her, anyone around her would always be in danger. That included Roy.

Kris was a sensible man. He was probably caught up in the high emotion of the situation they were in, just like she was. Right now she needed to be the calm and logical person. He'd offered that to her when she needed it; now she could offer it to him. Even if he didn't realize it was what was best for him.

His warm hand still rested on her cheek. Her heart fluttered despite her best intentions to keep it settled. A self-interested part of her wanted so badly to tell him that she hadn't chosen to leave Cedar Lodge because she *wanted* to. She felt emotionally torn in half. But she had to do the right thing. Her dad hadn't done the right thing, and look how much damage it had caused for so many people.

Dear Lord, please give me strength to make the best decision and follow through on it.

She reached up to rest her hand atop his. "I think Cedar Lodge is a dead end for me," she said. It wasn't a complete lie. It wasn't the complete truth, either. But dragging things out and hinting that they might have some kind of future together would be wrong.

She removed her hand and took a step back, letting his hand fall away from her cheek, not wanting to focus too much on the flicker of confusion in his eyes. Maybe he thought he knew how she felt. Maybe he was right. But if she didn't confirm it, it would be easier for him to let go of any closeness he felt for her and move on.

"I understand your worry for your family and concern for all of us," Kris said, his voice steady. "Maybe it's time to try to connect with your mom and tell her more about what's been going on. Find out if she's okay, too. Maybe that will help you decide to stay a little longer and keep trying."

So far, Monica had responded to her mom's texts with simple reassurances that she was okay. Monica had been worried her mom would relay her whereabouts to Nolan, either deliberately or unintentionally. But at this point, what did it matter? The bad guys obviously knew where Monica had been staying, and it was past time for her mom to face up to how dangerous the whole situation was. She'd indulged in denial long enough. Maybe relating the details of the attacks was the only proof Monica would ever have to show her mom that her fiancé was a terrible and dangerous man.

Monica took out her phone and sent her mom a brief text intended to start a conversation.

While waiting for a reply, she tapped the email icon on her phone to take a quick look at messages waiting in her inbox. The most recent item made her snap her head back in surprise.

"Something wrong?" Kris asked.

"It's from the office of my dad's lawyer. It's about the certified power of attorney I asked for. I thought they were going to call me and tell me if they'd be able to send it." Preparing herself for disappointment, she tapped the screen to open it. As she read, her breath caught in her throat. "It's here," she said. "They sent the power of attorney form."

Kris smiled. "I'll let Chief Ellis know we'll need a patrol car here in the morning so we can be at the bank as soon as they open."

Monica gave in to the impulse to reach out for a celebratory hug. Kris folded his muscled arms around her in response, and she pressed the side of her face against his chest. She could feel and hear the steady beat of his heart. Her own heart gave her away as it raced in her chest under the influence of his touch.

Kris didn't seem to be in any hurry to let go of her. And she wasn't anxious to leave his embrace, either. So she gave herself a few moments to enjoy it. This would be the last time they shared a moment like this one.

There was no guarantee there would even be a safe-deposit box at the bank belonging to her dad. Or that there would be anything helpful in it. And even if there was something that would keep her mom from marrying Archer and get her dad a reduction in his prison sentence, that wouldn't change things between Monica and Kris. She would still be the criminal's daughter whose family reputation would cast a shadow over Kris's career at the police department. She wouldn't be able to start her teaching career in Cedar Lodge, where the school board would discover her shady family connections. And most important of all, the Boyd Sierra syndicate would still hold a grudge against her, making it risky for anyone to be around her.

Slowly and regretfully, she let go of Kris. And she steeled her heart to the fact that no matter what happened at the bank tomorrow, she would be leaving Cedar Lodge, and she would not look back.

Monica stared down at the open safe-deposit box in front of her. She'd already picked up her grandfather's old pocket watch, her great-grandmother's engraved wedding ring, and a few other pieces of jewelry that had sentimental value for her dad. These must have been the final few belongings of monetary value her father owned that he would not sell to help pay for his legal defense after he'd been arrested.

Everything else had been cashed out to pay the lawyers.

A familiar shaking feeling started in the center of her chest. A sad sensation of loss and sorrow and disappointment for all she and her parents had been through and for the feeling that so much of her happiness as a child must have been built on a lie. She didn't really know her dad at all, never had. Her mother—not always the easiest relationship in her life—had become a stranger. And their shared history as a family seemed to have been reduced to these few objects.

Instead of sending a text reply last night, Suzanne had called her daughter. Torn by indecision, Monica had ultimately not answered the call. She was afraid that once she heard her mother's voice, she would say too much, potentially putting her mom or herself in danger. So she'd sent a text saying that she'd talk to her later.

Suzanne had left an angry voice message after that, but Monica had understood that it was fueled by fear. Whether it was fear for Monica or fear for herself, it was hard to say.

Here, now, inside a private area within the bank vault, Monica stared down at all that space where she'd hoped there would be data storage devices or photographs or documents or *something* that would tell her what she needed to know.

She tried to hold back the trembling sensation that came over her and blink away the tears. She shouldn't have gotten her hopes up. From the moment she left Reno for Cedar Lodge, she shouldn't have thought finding a resolution to all her family problems would be straightforward.

She left the items in the box and beckoned a bank employee to help her get the box secured again.

Disappointment hung heavy on her shoulders. She had no solid plans for what to do next. She and Kris had one more person they'd planned to talk to, Jason Mulhern, who owned the paving company that did work at the Elk Ridge Resort among other places. She was at a loss over what to do after that. It really did make sense for her to just leave town.

She spotted Kris in the lobby before he saw her. He was standing, his head moving slowly from side to side as he looked around the lobby and presumably out the windows at the surrounding streets of Cedar Lodge, keeping an eye out for potential attackers.

He turned to her just before she reached him, and the shift in his eyes to a sympathetic rather than vigilant expression made her realize that her own emotions must be clearly written on her face.

"What did you find?" he asked cautiously.

"Nothing helpful. A few pieces of jewelry." She shook her head. "There's no secret message attached to any of them or etched into the metal." She'd taken a close look at each item to make sure even though she'd felt foolish doing it.

"I'm sorry. I know this isn't what you'd hoped for. But we aren't at a point for you to give up hope or leave town just yet."

He gave her an encouraging smile, and despite her best intentions, she smiled back. She'd become too aware of the *moments* like this one that they'd shared. When their exchanges were beyond the objective sharing of information between a cop and a citizen in desperate need of help.

When had that even started? When had it all become so personal, this interaction between them? She'd been thinking about it since last night, and she still didn't know. Perhaps it had been that way from the beginning. But she couldn't let it continue.

She schooled her features, letting the smile fade away and keeping her voice impersonal and matter-of-fact as she said, "Hiding out and thinking only of myself isn't something I can live with. And if I'm not making headway here in Cedar Lodge, there's no reason to stay."

His gaze fixed on her, the warmth in his eyes fading. Within seconds he was wearing the cynical *cop face* expression.

She'd made her point. She'd pushed him away. He got the message.

He held up his phone and spoke in a professional tone. "I heard from Detective Campbell while you were in the vault. He's arranged a video meeting with a couple of parole officers who may have some insights into the thugs who've been attacking you."

Monica nodded uncertainly, not sure what kind of information he was talking about.

"Parolees sometimes pass on information to the officers managing their cases," Kris continued. "Since the parolees are out and about in the world, some of them pick up useful information. They're supposed to stay away from other criminals, but they don't always do that. And sometimes they share information with their parole officers. Chief Ellis wants me at the station to listen in. It's a secure meeting, so I can't have you attend. But I can tell you what I learn afterward. And we need to get going, because it's starting soon."

They walked outside. The bank was part of a commercial complex with shops and stores that spanned several connected buildings. They stepped out from a short passageway to the street, where a cop escort was waiting in a patrol car behind the Volker ranch SUV Kris had driven to the bank.

"Monica!"

Kris stepped closer to Monica, grasped her upper arm, and pulled her close to him.

Ryan Fergus walked up to them on the sidewalk. "Sorry, I probably shouldn't have yelled out your name like that," he said apologetically. "I'm just glad to see you in person and know you're all right."

"I'm okay."

"Good. Well, I'm actually here following up on some information that might help you."

"What's that?" Monica asked.

Ryan gestured toward a restaurant kitty-corner from where they stood. "I told you that I'd heard about a local business group with monthly luncheons that your dad sometimes met with. I think the Cedar Lodge Entrepreneur's Club might be that group. There's a meeting today at George's Farmhouse Restaurant over there, and I figured I'd check it out and see if it's the same one. I didn't want to mention anything until I knew for sure."

Despite herself, Monica got her hopes up. She was desperate for leads, and this was a plausible one. "I'll go with you," she said to Ryan. "Maybe I'll see someone I recognize or hear a familiar name."

"We need to get to the police station," Kris said, still holding her arm.

Ryan stepped back. "You don't need to go with me," he said to Monica. "Let me find out if your dad ever attended one of their meetings, and we'll proceed from there. If anybody has anything useful to say, I'll let you know immediately."

"You go to the police station," Monica said, gently disengaging her arm from Kris's grasp. "And I'll check out this entrepreneur's club."

Kris frowned at her.

She gestured at the officer in the patrol car. "Officer Anderson can keep an eye on me. And the police department is only three blocks away."

When Kris looked like he was not going to move, she started toward the cop car, and he followed. She gave the patrol officer a quick rundown of their plans. Then she turned to Kris. "*Please*, go so you don't miss the start of the meeting. After it's over we'll talk to Mulhern at his paving company shop. And if I learn anything at this meeting at the restaurant, we can follow up on that, too."

She felt energized by the prospect of getting somewhere.

"I don't like it," Kris said, crossing his arms. "Going in different directions."

"At this point, I'm potentially in danger anywhere I go. Even at your house. We might as well take advantage of every opportunity we get and try to follow up on leads as quickly as possible. My mom could marry Archer Nolan in a week, and I don't want that to happen. Ryan will be with me, and Officer Anderson will be keeping an eye on things. He can take me to the police station or back to the ranch."

Appearing hesitant, Kris apparently realized she wasn't going to give up, and he finally agreed. After leaning into the patrol car to say something to Anderson, he walked behind it to the SUV and got in. After a lingering look at Monica, he pulled away from the curb.

Monica glanced around the street, wondering if she'd ever again reach a point in her life when she didn't have to worry about her safety.

"Oh, I left my wallet in my car," Ryan said, patting his pockets. "I was planning to get something to eat while I was at the restaurant. They make fantastic omelets." He gestured toward the passageway behind them that led into the business complex. "If I cut through there, I can get to the side street where I parked my car a little quicker." He looked doubtful. "I don't know if you want to walk with me or wait in the patrol car?"

She didn't especially want to wait in the patrol car. And the side street he indicated was in the direction of the restaurant.

Ryan had already started through the passageway, saying something about Hunter Larson, but Monica couldn't hear it clearly.

She called out to the officer, who'd been

watching the whole time, "I'm going with him. We'll be right back."

She turned and hurried into the passageway to catch up with Ryan, who was still talking. She was walking beside him, trying to piece together exactly what he was saying about her dad, when she heard him make a strange sound.

And then everything went dark.

TWELVE

Kris strode out of the police station conference room, where the video meeting was still ongoing. The parole officers had reported none of their parolees knew anything about the attackers who'd targeted Monica, giving strong support to the idea that the assailants were professionals from out of town.

A couple of federal agents had joined the call, working with Detective Campbell on his attempts to track the thugs and tie the case to Boyd Sierra Associates. Kris was more interested in facts and leads that would specifically help to gather information that could help Monica's family. And at the moment, he was particularly concerned about Monica herself.

He'd regretted his decision to give in to Monica's request that they go their different ways the moment he'd driven away. Impatient to get back to her as quickly as possible, he'd interjected himself into the meeting and pushed the questions he and Monica needed answered. After learning that they had no specific leads, he decided it was time for him to go. He could catch up on any pertinent information later.

As he walked across the lobby, Jason Mulhern was at the forefront of his mind. He wanted to see for himself that Monica was okay, but she had a cop watching out for her, and Kris knew if he really wanted to help her, he would do everything he could to move the investigation forward.

The meeting had reminded him that Mulhern was the one specific person of interest he'd wanted to talk to but hadn't. The guy did have a criminal past, and it didn't necessarily follow that he was out of the game simply because there was nothing recent on his record. Maybe he just hadn't gotten caught. And Ryan had mentioned more than once that Mulhern seemed shady.

Rather than call ahead and give Mulhern time to fabricate lies or even slip out the back door, Kris decided to just drive to Mulhern Paving. He'd already looked at the location on his phone, and it wasn't far away.

He couldn't resist the temptation to call Monica on the way there. Of course, Anderson would have let him know if there was a problem. And dispatch would have alerted him in the meeting if something significant had happened. Still, he called.

She didn't answer. Pushing aside the shot of anxiety that threatened to overtake rational thought, he took a breath and sent a text: Everything okay? Maybe she'd found someone at the restaurant meeting who was offering her helpful information. Though at this point he wasn't clear on what that could possibly be. Computer files? Photos? Voice recordings? Or maybe it would be something completely different.

Monica had talked about her dad having found faith and changed for the better. And while Kris knew that was possible, his cop cynicism wouldn't go away. Maybe the furtive life of a mob accountant wasn't the only secret Hunter Larson had been hiding. Maybe that was why the criminals were so intent on getting to Monica.

He pulled up to a small metal prefab building with a sign reading Mulhern Paving attached to the side. It didn't appear to be a large business. He was about to reach for his police radio to check in with Anderson when an office door opened. A woman walked out and then locked the door behind her.

Kris saw only one vehicle in the parking lot. It appeared that if this woman left, there would be no one for him to talk to. He set aside the radio and got out to walk toward her. She gave him a friendly smile that faltered when he identified himself as a police officer.

"Can I help you?" she asked politely.

"I'd like to speak with Jason Mulhern."

"He not here. I'm Nancy Mulhern, his wife. What did you want to talk to him about?"

Kris glanced at the office window. Could Jason be listening and watching from behind the closed curtain? Had he and his wife seen Kris as he arrived? Perhaps Jason had seen Kris somewhere when Kris was in uniform. It would make sense for a criminal to remember the faces of most cops in town.

Kris didn't hear anything or see any movement around the window, so he turned his attention back to Mrs. Mulhern. "I need to ask your husband a few questions. I won't take much of his time."

"Have you got a specific crime you think my husband committed?" While not rude, she did sound defensive and somewhat annoyed.

"No, I'm not looking for him regarding a particular crime." He would need to see Mulhern and talk to him before he could begin to figure out where he might fit into all the criminal attacks.

Mrs. Mulhern made a scoffing sound. She shook her head and looked down before lifting her gaze again, holding her head slightly tilted. "Jason made some bad decisions fifteen *years* ago. He was twenty years old and desperate, and he paid for his mistakes. And he hasn't broken the law since. Yet whenever one of you cops gets stuck investigating a case involving a burglary or commercial theft and you can't find any solid leads, you come looking for my husband, hoping to pin it on him." She crossed her arms over her chest. "We've had enough of it."

Since Mulhern had served his sentence and completed parole long ago, Kris had no leverage to pressure the man to talk to him.

"There's a woman in town who's been the target of some vicious attacks," Kris began. "If you follow the local news, you've probably seen something about it."

The woman lifted her shoulders. "My husband would never be involved in anything like that."

Maybe, maybe not.

"I understand your husband has done a lot of work up at the Elk Ridge Resort. The woman who's been attacked has a connection to that location. Maybe your husband has seen something that would help with the investigation. Maybe he saw something and didn't realize its significance."

Or maybe he did more than just see something. Maybe he participated.

Kris especially wanted to find out if Mulhern was a general physical match for the assailants. Neither he nor Monica could make a specific match based on a photo of Mulhern because they hadn't gotten a good look at the assailants' faces.

"Please," Kris added. "It's important. Another attack could happen at any time."

His mind returned to worrying about Monica's safety since she hadn't responded to his call or text, giving him a coiling sensation in the pit of his stomach.

The woman sighed. "Jason got a call for an appraisal this morning. I don't know if he's still there or if he's finished that and gone on to check other projects." She pulled her phone out of her purse and tapped the screen. Kris could hear the call go through and start ringing on the other end. It went to voice mail. The woman left a brief message and disconnected. "He's obviously busy. I've texted him a couple of times this morning, and he hasn't responded yet."

"Where was the appraisal supposed to be done?"

"That old roadhouse east of town. People have said they were going to buy it and renovate it for years, but it looks as if Ryan Fergus is actually going to do it."

Ryan Fergus? The same Ryan who had repeatedly said he didn't trust Jason Mulhern and had pointed to him as a likely criminal? And also the same Ryan who was with Monica *right now*?

Monica hadn't responded to Kris's call or text.

Jason Mulhern hadn't responded to his wife's attempts to contact him.

Something was *very* wrong.

"Thank you," Kris called out as he turned and jogged toward the SUV, trying again to call Monica. When he got no response, he called Officer Anderson.

"Anderson," the officer responded when he answered.

"You have a visual on Monica right now, correct?"

"No. She and that friend you guys were with headed back toward the bank. They haven't come out yet."

"You didn't go with them?" Kris practically barked out the words.

"She didn't ask me to go with them. Just like she didn't ask me to go along the first time she went into the bank with you. I figured she had some private financial issue to take care of and after that they'd head over to the restaurant they were talking about."

Through the phone, Kris could hear the sound of a car door opening.

"I'm going inside the bank right now," Anderson said. He disconnected.

With Anderson headed into the bank to look for Monica, Kris made the snap decision to head for the county highway that would take him out to the roadhouse to see if Mulhern was still there. He started off in that direction.

Anderson called moments later. "Monica's not here. I'll head to the restaurant in case they ended up driving there in her friend's car and I didn't realize it."

"Make it fast," Kris snapped, furious that Anderson hadn't insisted on accompanying Monica wherever she went. It didn't matter that Anderson was technically right and he couldn't force his help on Monica. Kris gave him a quick summary of his plan to go to the roadhouse before disconnecting.

Monica, what were you thinking? Why hadn't she stayed with Anderson?

Kris did his best to corral his emotions. Monica wasn't a cop. She wasn't used to daily exposure to lies and deceit. She wasn't cynical. She'd known Ryan Fergus for a few years, and he must have seemed completely safe to her. Maybe he was a decent guy and the two of them had been taken by Mulhern. Or Brendan Stryker. Or the two hit men that had been dogging her all along.

Anderson called again. "Monica's not in the restaurant."

"Call Chief Ellis. Tell him what's happening and that we need to track Monica by her phone location." He knew the chief would automatically have dispatch issue a be-on-the-lookout for her. "I'll check in as soon as I get to the road-house."

Kris hit the gas pedal harder, already on the eastern edge of town where the highway opened up. He hoped and prayed that he would find Monica before it was too late.

Monica opened her eyes, her gaze fixed on the dusty concrete in front of her while she tried to figure out where she was and what had happened.

She was in a fairly large room that was shadowy and cool. She was lying on her side with her head resting on the concrete. She had a throbbing headache.

Ryan. The last thing she remembered was walking with Ryan. Was he here? Had he been kidnapped, too? It was obvious someone had knocked her out and brought her here.

She tried to push herself up into a sitting position, but found that her hands were tied behind her back. Her knees were bent, her ankles secured together with rope like her hands.

She must be in shock, because she felt concerned but not terrified. There wasn't the heart-pounding fear she'd experienced while being shot at or wrestling with an assailant trying to shove her into a fire. It was a strangely detached feeling. Maybe she'd just had all she could take and she was finally letting go.

No. Do not let go. Do not quit.

Where had those thoughts come from?

She knew the answer in an instant. From the part of her that had prayed and fought against despair after she'd been taken so low following her dad's arrest.

Dear Lord, please help me. I'm overwhelmed and tired. Of everything. But I know with You all things are possible. You can and will give me strength.

The prayer felt like it brought her back to her senses. Literally. Her wrists and ankles hurt. The concrete floor was colder. She felt *more* frightened.

She also felt more *alive*. And strengthened to do everything she could to stay that way.

She couldn't tell if there was anyone else in the room, watching her. What she could see from her awkward position was cabinets and metal doors and a pair of sinks on the other side of the room with a wide window above them, forest visible outside. There was also a set of ovens. So it must be a restaurant kitchen.

But the restaurant she'd intended to go to so she could question the entrepreneur's club about her dad would be busy and full of people right now. Not dusty and lit only by sunlight coming through the windows. Where was she?

Following an awkward series of movements,

she was finally able to get herself seated upright with her legs stretched out in front of her but her hands still behind her back. Her hair was in front of her eyes now, so she couldn't see much. She came to rest leaning against a cabinet that had a broken handle. Maybe she could use that to get her hands untied. Tilting her head, she blew out a puff of air to clear the hair from her eyes. She startled when she saw Jason Mulhern seated in a chair several feet away, staring in her direction.

Where was Ryan? Was he tied up somewhere in this building, too?

"You," she said to Jason. Her mouth was dry, and her throat was scratchy. "You're behind all of this? *You've* been trying to kill me?" She looked around, expecting to see an accomplice lurking in the shadows because it had been two men attacking her since she arrived in town.

He moved his head slightly and then said, "No, I haven't been trying to kill you." His words sounded awkward and distorted. She focused her attention more intently on him, and it became clear that he was slumped in the chair. That he was tied to it, actually. His lips were split, and there was blood at the corner of his mouth.

"What?" Her breath caught in her chest as the compulsion to *get out of here now* overtook her, and she was unable to force out any more words. She thought of the broken cabinet handle and pressed against it, hoping to use it to cut through the rope binding her hands.

"You're Monica Larson," he said with a scratchy voice. "I think I saw you at the resort, but I didn't recognize you at the time. It's been so long. I thought you looked a little familiar, but it took me a while to figure out why."

What was he talking about? It was hard to focus on him while trying to cut through the rope bindings on her wrists at the same time. She hardly knew what to say. But at such an extreme point, where her life might nearly be over, there was no reason not to talk blunt truth with him.

"I don't know you," she said. "I've heard you're a criminal. Maybe you've committed crimes with my dad." She shook her head. Acknowledging all that she'd learned about her father over the last year or so was still hard. "I came to Cedar Lodge hoping to find some information I think he wanted me to know. The criminal gang he used to work with is trying to kill me because they're afraid of what I might learn." She gave him a lingering look. "Does that mean you work for Boyd Sierra Associates, too? Are they now trying to kill you, as well?"

And if that was the case, why were they still both alive? Why hadn't the kidnappers already killed them?

"I have the information you're looking for," he said.

Was he lying to her? Was this some kind of trick?

In the quiet, while she tried to figure out what to do next, she heard cars driving by. Not heavy traffic, as if she were in the middle of town. But maybe enough that if she could just get outside, she could flag down help.

So far she hadn't accomplished anything using the broken handle behind her back. She couldn't get the metal edge lined up at the necessary angle to cut through the ropes. Frustrated, she looked around for some other way to get herself free as Jason started talking again.

"Your dad hid information in a folder inside an email account," Jason said. "He told me about it shortly before he went to prison. He told me how to access it and said he might someday send you to look for it."

"Okay, how do I access it?"

If she got out of here alive, maybe she would finally get what she'd been looking for. She still had so many questions. Why had her dad not told *her* how to access the information back when he was first arrested and before he was sent to prison? Why had he told Jason?

"First, we need to get out of here. Then I'll tell you everything," Jason said. "You can get up and move. I can't. I'm tied to this chair. Come this way and see if you can somehow untie these ropes."

She didn't trust him. What was his game? But then again, what other choice did she have?

She heard a male voice somewhere else in the building. There was no time to waste. She pulled hard on the broken handle, and it came off. Then she scooted across the cold concrete toward Jason. "I'm holding a broken handle I yanked off the cabinet door," she said. "Maybe it can cut through your ropes or pry them loose or something."

"I can move my hands a little," Jason said. "Give it to me, back up over here, and I'll try to cut your hands loose first."

Maybe he would do what he said. Or maybe he'd use the sharp edge of the broken handle to cut or stab her. In light of all that had happened, she wasn't inclined to trust him. But again, what other choice did she have?

"I'll have so many questions for you once we get out of here," she said.

"I'll tell you everything I know."

She gave him the handle, feeling him take a firm grasp of it with his fingertips. He quickly managed to slide it partially under the ropes that tied her. He began a sawing movement with it, using the sharp edge to cut the fibers.

At the same time, Monica tugged on the ropes as hard as she could. A wave of hope and relief passed through her when the rope finally loosened. Continuing to pull, she felt one hand slip free and then the other.

"Got it." She shook off the ropes.

Again she heard a male voice from somewhere else in the commercial kitchen. It was getting louder. The man was getting closer. Her stomach lurched when she finally recognized the voice and could make out the words. "Yes, you will pay me for her. And I've got a guy here we can kill and then stage the scene so it looks like he's the killer. I'll convince the cops that he grabbed Monica and forced me to come along since I was with her. I'll tell the police he was working with the two assailants they already know about. And I'll give them completely misleading descriptions."

Jason dropped the handle. "Help me get free."

Monica quickly pulled the rope off her ankles and then worked to get Jason's hands loose. They both hurried to get his feet untied and cast off the rope that had bound him to the chair.

As soon as he was free, he jumped up, knocking over the chair. The sound was loud in the nearly empty kitchen.

A door swung open, and Ryan hurried through holding a gun. He fired at Jason.

Jason dove behind the center island.

Terrified, Monica backed into a corner with nowhere to go. She heard a vehicle engine roar up to the building from the direction of the street.

"That would be the two gentlemen who have desperately been trying to eliminate you as a problem for their bosses," Ryan said in an even tone as if they were having a normal conversation. Even his facial expression was calm, almost as if he was simply taking a tour of the building.

He stepped farther into the kitchen, shifting his gaze back and forth between Monica and the area on the other side of the room where Jason had disappeared.

Heart pounding in her chest, Monica could barely hear the killers entering the building and striding toward them.

"It's nothing personal," Ryan said to Monica with a slight smile. "It's just business."

With that faint smile lingering on his thin lips, he turned at the sound of footsteps.

Kris appeared in the doorway with his gun drawn.

With a look of surprise and the smile finally wiped from his lips, Ryan immediately fired at Kris. The cop crouched and ducked back behind the doorway so that he was out of sight.

Ryan went after him, and Monica sprang forward from the corner of the kitchen. She grabbed the chair Jason had been tied to and swung it at Ryan, connecting with his head and causing him to lurch forward. He regained his balance and spun around while firing a wild shot at Monica. She dropped to the floor, and the bullet missed her.

Kris rushed through the door, and Monica jumped to her feet.

Ryan, now standing directly in front of Monica, faced off with Kris. If Kris fired, the bullet could hit Monica. Ryan could take advantage of that.

Monica was summoning her courage to jump on Ryan's back when Kris shifted his gun to his free hand and threw out a roundhouse punch that connected with Ryan's jaw. The older man spun, but righted himself and pointed his gun at Kris again.

"Drop it!" Kris yelled at the same time he threw out another punch, this time knocking Ryan out cold. Kris immediately grabbed the older man's dropped weapon.

Monica stepped up to wrap her arms around Kris. "We're okay," she said, her voice shaky. There were moments when she was sure she was not going to be okay. That she was going to die. And she'd had moments of the same worry about Kris.

He wrapped an arm around her and squeezed

her shoulders while keeping the other hand free so he could cautiously continue to point his gun at Ryan. Still, he managed to brush the top of her head with a kiss. "I wasn't going to stop until I found you."

Her knees nearly buckled with relief.

"Monica, are you okay?" Jason called out as he got to his feet on the other side of the kitchen island.

"Who are you?" Kris demanded, pointing his gun at the man who looked familiar.

"That's Jason Mulhern," Monica said. "Ryan kidnapped him, too."

Bang! Bang!

Before Monica could give any further explanation, shots blasted through the windows over the sink. Kris threw himself atop Monica, shielding her with his body. When the shots ended, Kris slowly got to his feet.

A second round of shots blasted through the window, and Kris hit the ground again. Monica closed her eyes tightly and covered her ears with her hands.

When this round of gunfire finally ended, Monica opened her eyes. A heavyset man had snuck through the doorway leading into the kitchen. He was the attacker who had tried to force her into the flames in the cabin fire. She knew it by the look of him and the way he moved.

The man snatched her wrist and yanked her to her feet before she could react.

In the instant it took for Kris to spin around and aim his gun at the assailant, the thug already had the barrel of his gun pressed against Monica's temple.

"Drop your gun," the criminal barked at Kris.

The cop shook his head. "Let her go."

"Drop your gun," the man repeated, grinding out the words. "Or I'll kill her right here in front of you. You know I'll do it."

Kris dropped his gun.

With his weapon still pressed against Monica's head, the attacker dragged Monica through the door of what she now recognized was the old roadhouse outside of town.

There was a van with its engine running in the gravel parking lot. The taller, skinny criminal Monica recognized from the cabin fire ran around from the back of the roadhouse. He must have been the person shooting through the window to draw away everyone's attention while the thickset guy snuck inside to grab Monica.

Kris stepped up to the doorway as the bad guy continued to drag her to the van while keeping his gun aimed at her head.

Why he or the other thug hadn't killed her on the spot, she didn't know. Maybe they were only keeping her alive so they could use her as leverage to escape from Kris.

No doubt once they got her into the van and drove away, her life would be over.

THIRTEEN

Kris heard footsteps coming up behind him and he turned his gun on the red-haired man who immediately held his hands up in a sign of surrender. "I'm not one of the bad guys. Ryan Fergus grabbed me and tied me up here before he kidnapped Monica."

Kris realized he'd seen a photo of the guy as well as his face on the Mulhern Paving company's website. "Jason Mulhern."

Jason gave a curt nod and cautiously put his hands down.

Kris had no idea what the former criminal was doing here or if he could even trust him, but grilling the man for information wasn't his highest priority at the moment. What he really cared about was the woman being taken away at gunpoint.

"I'll go out the back of the roadhouse and then come around the side and make a lot of noise," Jason said. "Maybe it will distract the guy holding Monica enough that he'll loosen his grip and you can get a clear shot at him."

It wasn't a terrible idea. Firing his gun any-where near Monica wasn't a *good* idea, but Kris couldn't risk them getting away and killing her before he could stop them. He held on to Ry-an's gun, still not trusting Jason enough to give it to him.

"Go!"

Kris heard Jason run back inside the road-house so he could go through and out the back. At the same time, he took aim at the criminal who clutched Monica's head in the crook of his arm while waving his gun and screaming threats at Kris. They were almost to the side door of the van.

The skinny assailant slid into the driver's seat. The second Monica was in the van, he would hit the gas pedal and they'd be gone. They might even kill her as soon as they were far enough away that Kris and his gun no longer posed a threat to them.

Kris stepped through the doorway onto the covered porch that ran the length of the road-house. The thug holding Monica yelled to his accomplice, and the skinny guy moved to open the door from inside the van.

Kris couldn't wait for Jason to create his distraction. For all he knew, the former thief had taken the opportunity to run away. So he locked gazes with Monica, who was staring at him, wide-eyed. There was a moment when he felt they understood one another. Maybe it was wishful thinking on his part. Maybe it was the continuing intensity of two people working so closely together in dangerous situations over the last few days. But the perception felt real. He was certain she understood he was about to do something drastic because they were beyond the point where they had any other choice.

The slider door began to open. Kris held Monica's gaze and gave a slight nod of his head. She mirrored the gesture. He took a breath and aimed his gun, ready to open fire.

"Hey! Let her go!" Jason popped his head around the corner of the building, waving his arms and yelling toward the attackers at the van before darting out of range.

In that moment, Monica lunged back from the criminal holding her, twisting away from the gun pointed at her head and ducking down.

Clearly aware that Kris was the greater danger to him, the attacker immediately fired at him.

Kris shot back.

Monica broke free from the kidnapper's grip. She began a stumbling run toward the side of the building and away from the line of fire as Kris and the kidnapper traded shots. From behind one of the porch's wooden posts, he glanced over to make certain she was okay.

Dear Lord, please protect her.

Meanwhile, the driver had slipped out of the van and started shooting at Kris, too.

As soon as Monica neared the corner of the roadhouse and the relative protection of the building, she turned to Kris as if checking to see that he was okay.

Run! he thought just before she disappeared from sight. He ducked behind the splintered porch railing and finally had a second to key his radio and call for help. He turned his focus back on the assailants, watching as both men clambered into the van and put it in Reverse.

Maybe they were admitting defeat.

But after backing a short distance, the driver shifted gears and barreled toward the side of the building where Monica had just been. The attackers weren't giving up. They were going after her until the bitter end.

Please let her have run into the woods.

There was a grassy area all around the old building where it had once been cleared for extra parking. But close to that, the ground became uneven and tilted downward into a wash. And there were trees everywhere. The van's engine was already making a grinding noise and sounded like it was no longer moving.

Were the bad guys already out of the van? Would they be waiting for him to chase after them?

He ran back into the roadhouse, through the dining and dance area and into the kitchen, where Ryan lay slumped on the floor, moaning. He continued out the back door, where he sprinted across a cracked concrete patio with a couple of broken-down picnic tables and beyond a swath of wild grass into the cover of the woods.

He looked through the dappled light, desperate to see a flash of color that matched Monica's clothes. Or even Jason's clothes. Anything to let him know where the two of them had gone. Because right now, he assumed the two of them were together.

Moving fast downhill through the shadowy forest, he quickly found the lowest part of the wash where it had a relatively even bottom and he could move at a fast pace. Years of search and rescue training had taught him that when people in the wilderness had no other plan, they typically moved downhill and took the path of least resistance.

He raced along, all the while scanning his surroundings, looking for broken tree branches or trampled plants or anything that might indicate which way he should go. He turned the volume down on his radio so the thugs wouldn't hear any of the transmissions. He'd given dispatch all the information they needed. At this point he was intent on rescuing Monica.

The assailants weren't visible, but he could hear them to his right and a little behind him. They were noisy in the forest and either not realizing or not caring that their voices carried as they spoke to one another, talking about which way Monica might have gone.

If these were the two men who'd attacked Monica at the cabin, they'd already demonstrated that they could track her in the woods. He sped up, feeling a rush of relief when he saw a small pine sapling with a recently snapped branch.

He stepped out of the wash into the cover of thicker trees and knelt to make himself less visible.

There, ahead of him behind a large deadfall tree, he saw leaves flutter where nothing else was moving. Maybe Monica was hiding back there.

The attackers had gone silent. There'd been no sound of a vehicle engine starting up, so Kris knew they hadn't driven away. Maybe they, too, had seen the wash and were following it right behind him.

Drawing closer to the downed tree lying on the ground, he caught a glimpse of Monica's booted foot. "It's Kris," he said as he approached, barely louder than a whisper. "Stay down," he cautioned. "I think they're nearby."

He rounded the fallen old tree, relieved to see Monica. He dropped down to the ground beside her. She was holding a tree branch, looking understandably wild-eyed. Beside her, Jason clutched a multipurpose tool with the blade extended.

"Are you okay?" Kris whispered.

Monica nodded. "I was worried you'd been shot."

"I'm fine." Kris could see a dark red mark on the side of her face. It looked like she'd been struck, and he pressed his lips together and felt a knot in his gut. Drawing in a steadying breath, he turned toward Jason.

"Have you got a plan?" Jason asked.

"Stay hidden until help arrives. Cops are on the way." What else could they do? Training and instinct combined with combat experience prodded him to take the offensive and go after the bad guys, but that could put Monica in greater danger. So they would wait.

As he lay there on the ground, Kris's senses were heightened. Not only was he looking and listening for the approaching criminals, but he was almost overwhelmingly aware of his determination to protect Monica. Keeping her safe was more important than his own safety. He glanced at her, admiring the determined set of her features. She'd been through so much, and she'd done everything she could to help her parents. She didn't deserve to be lying here in the dirt, fearful of losing her life.

The sound of snapping twigs behind them sent Kris spinning to face that way while still staying as low as possible. He pointed his gun in the direction of the sound.

Monica had also turned around, gripping her tree branch with both hands. Jason positioned himself with one foot and one knee on the ground, as if ready to sprint forward if needed.

The snapping noises sounded again, but they weren't very loud. Were they getting closer? It was hard for Kris to tell. Maybe if they were quiet, the thugs would continue on their way. He listened closely, and then he heard the much louder sounds of crashing branches coming from the direction of the roadhouse, the direction they'd originally been facing.

Kris spun back around in time to see the heavyset assailant moving forward, gun drawn. The criminal began shooting as he moved closer to them.

"Get down!" Kris called out. As the only one of them with a gun, he was the only one who stood a chance of stopping the shooter's deadly charge.

Kris fired a shot, and the thug ducked behind a tree, disappearing into the shadows only to suddenly reappear to Kris's right. The attacker was nearly to Monica, reaching out as if to grab her as she lifted the tree branch to defend herself. Kris had no choice but to shoot the man, his bullet striking him in the lower arm.

The creep grunted in pain and dropped his gun. When he reached down to retrieve it, Jason sprinted forward to grab it. As they grappled over the weapon the second thug dashed out of the woods from a different direction.

Kris looked up to see the skinny criminal pointing a gun at him.

Before the assailant could fire, Monica swung her tree branch and hit him in the face. Kris jumped the guy, quickly pinning him to the ground with his knee in the center of the man's back. He glanced over to confirm that Jason had the injured attacker's gun so that both men were subdued.

Sirens sounded in the distance.

"Grab my radio," Kris said to Monica. "It's attached to my belt. You'll need to turn on the volume."

For a moment, she just stared at him. He wouldn't blame her if she was in shock.

"It's going to be okay," he said calmly. "But I don't want to let go of this jerk and risk him getting away. We need to let the officers know where we are."

Monica reached for the radio, her hand trembling from the fear and adrenaline still overwhelming her mind and body. She keyed it, identified herself, stated that she was with Officer Volker, and then began describing what had happened and where they were located. In the distance it sounded like the initial responders were pulling into the roadhouse parking lot. Seconds later, she heard the cops reporting their arrival to dispatch.

Shifting her gaze between Kris and Jason as they kept control of the criminals, Monica offered up a silent prayer. *Thank You, Lord.* The long list of specifics she was thankful for would probably be in her mind for the rest of her life. For now, she was mostly grateful that she and Kris and Jason were alive.

She heard the sound of breaking branches and snapping twigs coming downhill in their direction. When she saw a flash of dark blue police uniform between the trees, she called out, "We're over here."

It seemed as if the three Cedar Lodge police

officers, and Kris's deputy friend Dylan, appeared in an instant, guns drawn, looking grim.

"Kris, are you and Monica all right?" Cole was behind them carrying his paramedic gear, with an EMT in tow.

"Yeah, we're okay," Kris said. "I shot one of the perps in the arm, so you'll need to assess that. There's also an assailant inside the roadhouse who was knocked out. The last I saw of him, he was unconscious."

Ryan Fergus. The shock of discovering he'd betrayed Monica hadn't yet worn off. Beyond being a surprise, it made no sense. He'd had so many opportunities to kill her. Why hadn't he completed the job?

The EMT and one of the cops headed back up toward the roadhouse to see after Ryan.

Watching them go, Monica felt her initial sense of relief dissipate. There were still so many unanswered questions about everything, not only Ryan's role in the attacks. Did Jason Mulhern actually have information entrusted to him by her father? Would it be significant enough to make any difference, and would it be enough to stop the Boyd Sierra syndicate from hounding her? And why would her father hide whatever it was with Jason and not with his own daughter? In the end, capturing these two goons—and

Ryan—solved the most pressing issues of the attacks against her, but it didn't solve everything.

She turned to Kris, who had just handed over the assailant he was restraining to one of the officers. He locked gazes with Monica, and for a moment they just stared at each other. And then he smiled.

Heartbreak radiated from Monica's head to her toes. Kris Volker was such a good man. A kind and loving man. A *family* man. And yes, a handsome man. Everything she'd ever wanted.

But wrapping up this particular battle didn't put a complete end to the danger that had been stalking her. There were still potential threats looming on the horizon and unanswered questions. And that meant if she pursued a relationship with Kris, she would put not only him in danger, but potentially his son and his parents, as well.

Kris stepped forward through the tall grass and wrapped his arms around her.

Despite her earlier determination to hide her feelings, she clung to him in return, giving herself this moment to feel the reassurance of his muscular arms wrapped around her and the comfort of hearing his heart beat steadily in his chest.

She looked up at him and he leaned down for a kiss, the tender press of his lips against hers making her heart skip several beats as a warm blush raced over her skin.

They'd survived this together. The creeps who'd tried to kill her the night she'd first arrived in Cedar Lodge and several times after were in custody. That was something to celebrate. She would relish the accomplishment and let herself enjoy the feeling of being held in Kris's arms for the moment.

But she couldn't deny reality forever. That would be too dangerous.

"We did it," Kris said.

"Yes, we did."

"I was afraid I was going to lose you."

She looked away, knowing exactly what that declaration meant. The words were right there on the tip of her tongue, ready to be said back to him. She cared about Kris. *A lot.*

"I was afraid for you, too," she finally said, regretfully pulling away from him. "That was some kind of Wild West shooting, cowboy. Both when we were up there in front of the roadhouse and then afterward when we got ambushed here, too."

She forced a wide smile on her lips and offered a challenging lift of her chin. She would shift the tone from a romantic connection to something more like friends.

"Thanks." Kris's expression seemed to sadden before her eyes. She'd hurt him by not responding the way he'd wanted her to. An ache formed in her chest that she quickly identified as sorrow for having seemingly rejected him. She reminded herself that he would look and feel infinitely more hurt if a new set of criminals came after her and Roy got caught in the crossfire.

She really did love Kris. It was impossible not to. And because she loved him, she wanted to protect him and his son.

The injury to the kidnapper Kris had shot was not life-threatening. Cole and an officer helped the man up the incline toward the flat ground at the roadhouse where the criminal could be put into an ambulance. The other bad guy had already been handcuffed and walked up to one of the patrol cars.

"Well, this kind of thing has happened enough times that I already know I'll have to give an official statement, and you'll need to write a report."

Kris nodded. "You are correct."

As Monica started to walk beside him back toward the roadhouse, she moved unsteadily. "My knees are wobbly. I'm not sure why."

"Residual adrenaline," Kris said.

He offered his hand, and Monica clasped it. Didn't matter what her brain told her about shuttering any romantic feelings she had for him.

Her stubborn heart did a little dance in response to his touch anyway.

She tightened her hold on him, knowing that it wouldn't last for long. Her time in Cedar Lodge was just about wrapped up.

FOURTEEN

Kris pulled his SUV into the police station parking lot the following morning with Monica seated beside him.

They'd been here yesterday afternoon, giving statements about the kidnapping and shooting at the roadhouse. But after a couple of hours during which all three perps were uncooperative and information was not forthcoming, Chief Ellis had told them to go back to the ranch with the assurance that he'd fill them in on the pertinent details when he finally had them.

Early this morning, Kris had gotten a text from Ellis asking Kris and Monica to show up for a meeting with Detective Campbell and Jason Mulhern at ten o'clock. Kris and Monica had not spoken with Mulhern after the arrests at the roadhouse when he'd been taken aside to give his own account of what had happened.

"I don't know why, but I feel nervous about this," Monica said as Kris parked and killed the engine. "I guess because the last twenty-four hours has been so overwhelming. It's hard to process all that's happened."

"If you want me to take you back to the ranch, I will," Kris offered. It would probably scare her if he told her he would do pretty much whatever she wanted if it made her happy. Even let her cut him out of her life and head back to Reno.

Monica had been quiet and emotionally distant when the two of them were at the police station yesterday. Even more so after they'd gone back to the ranch. She'd avoided him beyond making polite conversation when the family sat down for dinner.

Kris knew something of the struggle to process difficult emotions, and it was plain that Monica still had a lot to work out about her dad and her relationship with her mom.

In some ways, Kris would always be emotionally processing the sad passing of his late wife. He didn't want to forget about her. And he was determined to talk about her around Roy so that his son could have some feeling that he *knew* her. The boy's actual memories of his mother were sparse and mostly impressions rather than specific events or even what she looked like.

Could Monica accept that? He didn't know. But he would like to. And if he were going to be selfish, he wanted her to stay in Cedar Lodge. For his own sake as well as his son's.

After nearly losing Monica—more than once— he finally understood to the core of his being that the best thing he could do for his late wife's memory was to continue on with a full life for their son as well as himself.

And he wanted to explore what a full life with Monica might be like. He'd never met another woman like her. He'd been afraid that if he got seriously involved with someone, he would compare her with his late wife. And he had made the comparison, a little bit, at first. But the more he knew Monica, the more she was completely her own woman in his mind. And surprisingly, he didn't feel guilty about his growing feelings for her.

He hopped out of the truck and walked around to open Monica's door for her. Habit had him glancing around, just to make sure it was safe.

Inside the police department, they headed for the largest conference room. Chief Ellis and Detective Campbell were there, along with Jason Mulhern.

"We've already interviewed Mr. Mulhern," Chief Ellis said to Monica. "He told us there were some things he had to say, and he wanted to make sure you heard them."

"I'm curious to know what information you

have about my dad," Monica said to Jason as everyone was seated. "But I'm a little bit afraid to find out what it is, too." She turned to Kris with a faint smile and rubbed the side of her head. "I *still* don't remember what my dad said to me during that prison visit before the car crash. I guess I never will."

Jason turned to Monica. "I want you to know that I wasn't intentionally trying to hide anything from you." He glanced at Ellis for a moment as if wanting to confirm that the chief acknowledged what he was saying. "I own my business," he continued, addressing Monica. "I've got a family. Four children. My wife says I'm a workaholic, and maybe I am. I don't keep a close eye on the news, so I didn't know you were attacked here in town. When I saw you at the resort, I didn't realize you were Hunter Larson's daughter. You were a kid the last time I saw you." He offered her a slight smile. "Ryan Fergus contacted me and asked if I'd meet him at the roadhouse and give him an estimate on what it would cost to pave the parking area and the patio in back, so I did. One minute we were talking in the kitchen. The next I was waking up after he'd apparently knocked me out and tied me up. Later, he carried you in and set you on the floor. Between overhearing him on his phone mentioning Monica

Larson and looking at you lying there, I realized who you were."

"Who are you to my dad?" Monica asked. "Why would he hide information with you instead of me? What did Ryan have to do with this?"

"When I was younger, I was desperate for money, and I did some stupid things," Jason said with a shake of his head. "After I got out of lockup, the only job I could get was cleaning up the gym at the resort. I met your dad, and we'd chat a little once in a while. That's when I saw you and your mom sometimes. It's not like we were best buddies, but when I told him my story, your dad said encouraging things to me. Stuff that gave me hope that I could turn my life around."

Kris glanced at Monica and saw her smiling softly. At least she would get to hear one good thing about her dad today. It sounded like he was basically a kind man.

"Anyway, Mr. Larson and I met a few times for lunch over the years when he was in town." This time Jason turned his gaze to Kris and Detective Campbell and then to Chief Ellis. "I was shocked when he contacted me a little over a year ago and told me I was the only person he could trust with some information. That he was going to prison. Maybe for a long time."

"He didn't trust me?" Monica said sadly.

"He didn't want to put you in a position where you'd have to lie or hide anything for him," Jason said. "He told me I could opt out of holding on to the information for him, but I felt I owed him, and I wanted to help. It was simple enough. He'd set up an email account with several dummy folders with random stuff in them, and one significant folder had all kinds of important information in it. He gave me the email address and the login and password. He told me that you or your mom might come to me one day and ask for it, and I should help you."

"Of course you took a peek at it," Kris said.

Jason shook his head. "I was tempted to at first. But when my wife told me about Mr. Larson being in the news down in Reno—we kept track of him over the years since he'd been so kind—I realized he was connected to organized crime and I decided to stay out of it."

"So, what was in there?" Monica asked.

Jason gestured toward Detective Campbell. "That's what I'd like to know. I told the police last night how to access the information your dad had hidden."

"There's a lot in there about Boyd Sierra Associates," Campbell said with a broad smile. "Banking information. Summaries of many of their illegal operations. Names of members and descriptions of crimes they committed. Government employees and justice system employees on their payroll. Photos and voice recordings. I've shared it with my colleagues in federal law enforcement who have been working with me since the initial attack on you in Cedar Lodge. Specifically because of the suspected organized crime connection. They'll be combing through everything and getting ready to take down the top-level bad guys."

"What about Archer Nolan, my dad's *friend* who swooped in and swept my mom off her feet?" Monica's tone was steeped in sarcasm. "Is there anything about him in there?"

Campbell nodded. "He's in the notes. There are photos of him with known thugs. Voice recordings of him giving directions for crimes. A warrant is being issued for his arrest."

"Should be enough to convince your mom," Kris said. He knew how important that had been to her.

She sighed heavily. "I hope so." Then she turned to Chief Ellis. "So, what's next? Do you think the Boyd Sierra people will keep coming after me? Especially after some of them start getting arrested. They'll know you got the information because of me, and they'll be furious."

"The ones who are most furious will be the ones who are locked up," Campbell interjected.

"And the ones who aren't locked up will be busy lawyering up and covering their tracks."

"What these kind of people do isn't some impulse crime spurred by emotion," Ellis added. "They're coldhearted businesspeople. Chasing you down or hiring someone to do that would be a waste of resources and make them vulnerable to further charges. I think they'll be busy for a while. There won't be anything for them to gain by coming after you at this point. Their goal in attacking you was to prevent all of this criminal information from getting to the authorities. Obviously, it's too late for that now. As a practical matter, I think they'll cut their losses and leave you alone."

Kris watched Monica's face for a reaction, hoping she'd turn to look at him. If this case was closed, at least for her, did that mean she would consider staying?

He thought he'd already indicated clearly enough how he felt about her. But maybe he needed to do more. *Say* more. They'd been through so much together under such stressful circumstances that they hadn't been able to focus on each other personally.

"What about Ryan Fergus and the two thugs who have been after me since I arrived in town?" Monica asked the police chief.

"Ryan quickly got a lawyer, and they immediately negotiated a plea deal. So he's already talking. He claims he was never employed by the Boyd Sierra people, but he'd met a few of them while working on buildings owned by them when he still lived in Reno. Part of the reason he and your dad chatted was that, professionally, they traveled in some of the same circles. When you showed up in town and the attacks started, he had a feeling they might be connected to your dad being on the outs with the Boyd Sierra syndicate.

"It took him a few days to connect with someone in Reno because he wasn't part of their organization. He didn't try to contact their hit men in town, but not because he was afraid of them. Actually, he was in competition with them. He wanted to grab you first and get paid for delivering you to them. They were willing to pay him if he got to you before their thugs did. So he formed his plan, which included making it look like Mr. Mulhern had kidnapped you and then been murdered by unidentified assailants. Ryan intended to have it appear to the authorities that he'd been kidnapped and physically assaulted, too.

"In the end, the thugs in town had been contacted to meet up with Ryan at the roadhouse and take custody of you."

"And kill me."

Ellis nodded. "Most likely. I think the only reason they didn't kill you at the roadhouse was that they were afraid of getting shot by Kris."

"Are either of the two assailants talking?" Kris asked.

"Not yet," Ellis said. "I'm sure they're more afraid of their employers than they are of going to prison." He got to his feet. "Now, Campbell and I have got a lot of work to do." He turned to Kris. "You'll be back to work your regular shift tomorrow, right?"

"Yes, sir." Now that he thought the family ranch would be a safe haven again, he was anxious to get his son and bring him home. He glanced at Monica as everyone stood and began exiting the conference room. It would feel more like a home—for him and his son—if Monica were there, too.

He had to know if she would give him and Roy a chance. If she would linger in town long enough to find out if the connection they felt was real.

"I'll book an airline ticket back to Reno and then get a rideshare out to the airport," Monica said as Kris made the turn onto the drive up to the house at the Double V Ranch.

When they'd gone past the nearby road up to the Bennett cabin a few moments ago, she'd expected to feel that familiar twist of anxiety in her gut and the reminder of all the danger she'd been subjected to. But she hadn't. Instead, surprisingly, she'd felt a sense of completion. At least when it came to the dangerous Boyd Sierra Associates.

There were still so many things in her personal life that remained disordered and chaotic. She *had* to go back and take care of them. Even though what she most wanted in her life was right here beside her. Kris Volker was a man with deep roots in Cedar Lodge, Montana. He wasn't going anywhere.

She held her breath for a moment, hoping that Kris would ask her to stay. But he didn't. Trying to focus on gratitude for all he'd done rather than disappointment that he didn't want to pursue a relationship with her, she pasted a quivering smile on her lips and said, "Thank you for all your help." She kept it short so there was less chance of her bursting into tears.

"What do you need to do back in Reno?" he finally asked.

They were parked now and getting out of the truck.

"There's a lot of stuff I've got to work out with both my parents." Maybe by now her dad was allowed to have visitors again. And the conversation she'd have with her mom when she arrived back in town would be complicated, to say the least. "I don't know how grateful my mother will be for all of our efforts after Archer is arrested. I'm confident in time she'll appreciate having her criminal fiancé unmasked, but at first, not so much."

"And what happens after that? After you get your *stuff* worked out?"

He held his hand out to her. It was a small gesture physically, but it was big in meaning since it appeared to express a desire for a romantic relationship now that their working partnership was over.

Monica felt a cautious flutter in her heart as she took his hand. She was afraid to hope, but she couldn't help it.

To her surprise, rather than walking to the house, Kris led the way to the stables and the nearby corral where several horses languidly nibbled grass. She hadn't seen much of the stables—or the ranch at all, really—because people had been trying to kill her. It had seemed sensible to stay inside the house when she wasn't out with Kris trying to get her awful family predicament sorted out.

"What happens after I talk at length with my mom and dad?" she responded. "I don't know. I figure out how I'm going to restart my life, I guess."

He laughed softly. Confused, she turned to look at him.

"Restarting your life sounds like a good thing. It's something I've needed to do for a while, too. In some ways, my life stopped when Angela passed away. And it didn't start again until I met you."

Her heart pounded almost painfully in her chest. When she'd thought her investigation was putting his family at risk and that it might have reached a dead end anyway, she'd told him it was time for her to go. He'd asked her to stay, and she'd rebuffed him. She'd known it had hurt him, but it had felt like the right thing.

After the dust had settled at the roadhouse yesterday and the three perps were arrested, she'd had second thoughts about leaving. Fact was, she realized she wanted to continue to have Officer Kris Volker by her side. All the time. But she figured she'd ruined her chance. And that weighed heavy on her heart.

She felt at home on this ranch. Kris's parents had been so kind to her, and his friends Cole and Dylan had joked with her a little and treated her like a buddy even though she'd known them such a short time.

What she wanted for the rest of her life, what she'd always dreamed of, was right here. Most especially in the form of the man standing beside her at the corral railing while they watched the horses.

She looked at her hand, still clasped by his. She understood what he was indirectly asking her, just like she'd understood so much about him almost from the beginning. It seemed only fair that she take her turn and admit her true feelings. She gathered her courage. Her life had been on the line, and now she had to willingly put her heart out there.

"I need to leave for a while," she said, giving his hand a squeeze. "But I'd like to have a reason to come back."

He turned to her, lifting an eyebrow. "Would you, now?"

She'd made herself vulnerable and he was going to tease her? *Really?*

But then he let go of her hand and wrapped his arms around her instead, holding her loosely and gazing down at her face. "I want you to have a reason to come back here, too." He lifted a hand to her cheek, trailing a finger along the line of her jaw.

Monica sighed deeply, the fluttering sensation in the center of her chest combining wonderfully with a feeling of safety and certainty she hadn't felt in a long time.

Kris leaned down to gently press his forehead to hers. She pulled him closer, and he moved in for a lingering kiss that was warm and tender. Monica held on to him for several moments after the kiss ended, enjoying the sheltering feeling of his arms wrapped around her and the solid certainty of him holding her tight.

"Being associated with the daughter of a mob accountant could harm your career," she said hesitantly. "Are you sure you're okay with that?"

He replied with a half smile. "People can always find a reason to be critical if they want to. Beyond that, anybody who cares about me or works with me knows what kind of man I am. And when they see us together, they'll figure out what kind of woman you are, too."

"And Roy?" She knew his little boy was his number one priority, as he should be.

Kris's smile broadened at the sound of his son's name. "Roy has a big heart. He looks for reasons to like everybody. He'll be back here at the ranch later today." He shook his head. "My kid sounds like he doesn't want to leave his grandparents' house, and I'm a little sore about that." It was clear by his tone that he was joking.

His smile faded slowly, and his tone became more serious. "For his sake, we'll need to take things slow. Which might be a nice change since things have moved so fast from the moment I first saw you."

That might seem like it lacked excitement

to someone else, but not to her. After so many betrayals—from her father turning out to be a criminal to Ryan Fergus attempting to exchange her for payment from the killers—a slow and steady building of trust sounded like just what her heart needed to heal.

"Slow can be good," she said after a moment.

"I agree." He leaned in for a slow and toe-curling kiss.

Monica had no doubt that as soon as she got things wrapped up in Reno, she'd get back to Cedar Lodge and the Double V Ranch as fast as she could.

EPILOGUE

One Year Later

"I love you," Kris said, his dark blue eyes filled with emotion.

"I love you, too." Monica closed her eyes as Kris leaned in for a kiss, enjoying the moment. She'd spent the day savoring moments. It began with putting on her wedding dress and was followed by walking down the aisle and then seeing Kris in his tuxedo waiting for her with Roy in a matching tuxedo beside him. After that she'd felt humbled by the solemnity of the moment when she and Kris exchanged rings and the pastor had pronounced them husband and wife.

After the kiss ended, Kris moved until he was beside her, his arm across her waist. They were standing at the end of a pier at Bear Lake. The wedding reception was being held at a lakeside venue across the street from the church where they'd exchanged their vows. Esmeralda had provided the flowers from her own gardens. And now everyone was relaxing, enjoying themselves.

Roy in particular seemed to be having an especially good time. He let out a squeal, and Monica glanced over to watch him and his cousins and young friends race around and play in the lakeside grass. The sounds of mellow instrumental music could be heard. It was dusk, and stars were visible in the purple-blue sky. Fairy lights twinkled from the venue's outside dance floor as well as the railings on the pier. Cole and Dylan were both dancing with their dates for the evening.

For the first few weeks after the attacks on her a year ago, Monica had experienced brief flashbacks of the most harrowing moments. But the occurrences had slowed, and the accompanying anxiety had eased until it finally vanished. Spending lots of time with Kris and his friends and family had helped with that.

So had getting a chance to talk with her dad and tell him about the events. She still hadn't recovered her memory of that pivotal meeting with him at the prison, but he did confirm that he'd told her to contact Jason Mulhern in Cedar Lodge, Montana. She missed having her father at her wedding, but she was determined to focus on the future. And right now it looked especially good.

Monica's mom had been present when Archer Nolan was arrested. Once she got past the shock, she'd been appreciative of all Monica had done. Their relationship had gotten closer over the last year, and her mom was here now. While some of the relationships in Monica's life had been wildly irregular, she'd come to realize that all strong relationships came with problems and challenges and the need for forgiveness on both sides.

A small Christian school in town had been willing to hire Monica on Kris's and Esmeralda's recommendations. That had allowed Monica to rent a small apartment in Cedar Lodge while she and Kris—and Roy—all began to get to know each other better.

Monica and Kris had fallen in love quickly, but they'd given it time. Mostly for Roy's sake.

Monica now had the kind of life she'd dreamed of. It had needed time to take shape, but it was here now. She finally had the love and the family and the sense of belonging that she'd always longed for.

She and Kris remained standing, side by side, until it almost felt as if they'd melted together into one person, both helping to keep the other strong and upright. After a few moments, Monica realized she heard a commotion behind them. She and Kris turned around. The wedding guests on the outside dance floor were waving at them and yelling their names.

"Hey, come on back and dance!" Cole called out to them with his hands cupped around his mouth.

"Kris has two left feet, but you're stuck with him now!" Dylan added.

The dance! Between greeting guests and keeping track of Roy and then eating some dinner and cutting the cake, they hadn't had their first dance yet.

Beside her, Kris was laughing. "You realize you're stuck with all of us now, right?"

She leaned in for a quick kiss. "I wouldn't have it any other way."

Hand in hand, they strode from the end of the pier toward the lake's grassy shore. When they got there, Roy raced over to tackle his dad. Kris picked him up and set him on his shoulders. Then he reached for Monica's hand.

Monica smiled, feeling the warmth of the moment settle in her heart. Here was *another* moment to savor. And she had no doubt there would be many, many more such moments to come.

* * * * *

Dear Reader,

Life hands all of us troubles and challenges. There's no getting away from that.

I don't know why so many of us hesitate to ask for help, but we do. Maybe it's because we don't want to be a bother. And yet helping someone is *a blessing to the helper* as well as to the recipient of that help. It lifts our spirits to assist another person who needs us. Or a critter who could use our help.

Deadly Ranch Hideout is the first book in the Big Sky First Responders series. This series is about four high school friends who served in the military and are now back in civilian life helping others as their chosen careers. They know the power of doing something for someone in need and standing beside that person when they're in danger or facing tragedy. And sometimes they need a reminder that they can have a romantic life, too. I hope you'll join me for all four stories.

I invite you to visit my website, jennanight.com, where you can sign up for my newsletter. You can also keep up with me on my Jenna Night Facebook page or get alerts about upcoming books by following me on BookBub. My email address is jenna@jennanight.com. I'd love to hear from you.

Jenna Night